"NOTHING HAPPENED"

Mr. Ferranto holds up his hand. "Listen to me, all of you. If you know what's best for you, you'll tell me exactly what took place on the third floor. You are not going to get out of this by playing games with me."

"Nothing," Brig says.

"I don't want to hear 'nothing' again Mr. Briggers, Mr. Wingate, Mr. Candrella." Mr. Ferranto leans forward, speaking slowly. "I hope you understand how serious this is. Do you understand that you can be expelled from this school ... that this can go on your record and that every college you apply to will see that on your record? Do you understand that your whole life might be changed by your mean and thoughtless actions?"

There is silence.

Other Avon Flare Books by
Norma Fox Mazer

AFTER THE RAIN
BABYFACE
DOWNTOWN
MRS. FISH, APE, AND ME, THE DUMP QUEEN
SILVER
TAKING TERRI MUELLER

OUT OF CONTROL

NORMA FOX MAZER

AN AVON FLARE BOOK

AVON BOOKS
A division of
The Hearst Corporation
1350 Avenue of the Americas
New York, New York 10019

Copyright © 1993 by Norma Fox Mazer
Published by arrangement with the author
Library of Congress Catalog Card Number: 92-32516
ISBN: 0-380-71347-0
RL: 5.0

First Avon Flare Printing: April 1994

AVON FLARE TRADEMARK REG. U.S. PAT. OFF. AND IN OTHER COUNTRIES, MARCA REGISTRADA, HECHO EN U.S.A.

Printed in the U.S.A.

RA 10 9 8 7 6 5 4 3 2 1

Once again, for Harry,
dear friend and companion of my life.

Hello, this is Rollo Wingate speaking on a cassette recorder—

How am I going to do this?

Just start talking, I guess. Okay, here's the thing. What happened that day in school is sort of on my mind. I mean it *is* on my mind—

Wait. I feel nervous talking about this. I'm going to close the door.

Okay.

Start again. Uh, hello, this is Rollo Wingate speaking on his cassette recorder. It's Christmas vacation, and I'm lying on the floor of my bedroom with my eyes closed and I'm sort of nervous. I'm going to try to tell what . . . what, uh, happened that day.

I don't know what to call it. It wasn't what my father said. It wasn't an assault. We didn't beat her up or rape her or anything. It wasn't like that. It was just . . . it was something we did and, like Candy said, it got a little out of hand.

That's one good thing about Candy, he can take a situation and say something about it so you feel reassured. Like that time a few years ago when we were thirteen and wanted to go swimming in the quarry. We hid our bikes in the underbrush on Tower Road and climbed over the gate United Gravel had put up. Candy was pissed about the gate. He's lived in Highbridge all his life and nobody ever kept him out of the quarry before. It was a hot day. We went across the field toward the quarry. The guardhouse they'd put up was empty. We pried a window open in back and climbed in.

It was just one little room with a cot and a stove and a desk. It was so hot the flies were dying against the windows. "We could bring girls here," Candy said, and we laughed like a couple of maniacs.

All of a sudden, we heard men's voices. It sounded like they were right outside. I almost pissed my pants.

We scrambled and hid under the cot until they went past. "What if they'd caught us?" I said.

"If they left the stupid place unlocked, nobody would have to break in," Candy said.

And I thought, Yeah! That's right!

It was exactly the way I felt when Candy said that things got out of hand with her. I thought, Yeah, right! And I felt relieved.

I wish I could forget it, though.

I called Brig the first day of vacation before he left for Florida with his family. He said, "Rollo, baby! What's up?"

"Not much. How about you?"

"Everything's okay."

"Brig, are you thinking about it?"

"Thinking about what?"

"You know. Her."

"I don't have any hers on my mind, Rollo."

"I mean, what happened—"

"Nothing happened, Rollo."

"Brig—"

"You hear me, Rollo? You listening? I'm telling you, just like I told Mr. Principal, just like I told my father, nothing happened. She's a bigmouth and a liar."

* * *

Okay, time out. I'm going down for something to eat.

Here I am again. Maybe I should tell something about myself. Maybe someone is going to hear this tape someday and they'll want to know, Who is this guy? What kind of person is he?

That's what my father said. "What kind of person are you? Are you my son?"

Shit.

Okay, okay, I don't want to think about that now. Describe myself. Right. I'm a big guy. I've been big ever since, well, ever since I can remember. Bigger than everyone from kindergarten on. I'm built wide, broad in the beam. I've got big arms, big legs, big bones, big hands, big feet. Everything's big except my mouth. I've got a little mouth, like a girl's. I don't like that. I don't like saying it.

In grade school, everyone always wanted me on their team, and the team that didn't get me, the guys would run into me and hit me as hard as they could. Every guy wanted to be the one to knock me over. They'd say, "You love it, don't you, Rollo?" And I'd say, "Yeah!" But it scared me. It scared me when guys screamed and got this look on their face, excited, sort of like dogs, grinning the way dogs grin.

I remember when I met Brig and Candy. It was the summer after my mother died, and we had just moved to Highbridge. The bell rang, I went to the door, and I saw a little guy and a taller, freckled guy. "He's a monster," the little guy said, staring at me. The tall one with the flat, freckled face grinned. "Don't listen to anything Brig says."

The two of them started punching each other. Then we went out and played football on the lawn. Brig kept trying to get past me. He was the same then as he is now, like steam spouting out of a kettle, always moving, always going for it, always pushing. And Candy—just like now, he had a way of blowing off Brig, sometimes laughing at him, sometimes calming him down. It had always been him and Brig, but they let me in, and we did everything together from then on.

My father told me Candy's father was State Senator Candrella. "A big shot," I said, sort of impressed. Candy didn't act like a big shot, though, unless it was the way almost nothing seemed to bother him. He was the one who gave us a name. The Major Three. In seventh grade we changed it to the Lethal Threesome. In ninth grade we all agreed, Let it drop, we're too old for that crap.

But a few months ago, when the high school paper

did a Stars of the Junior Class feature, they posed us together in the gym and printed the picture with LETHAL THREESOME underneath. In parentheses under Candy, they wrote MR. PREZ OF STUDENT SEN-ATE; and under me, MR. STOMP OF FOOTBALL TEAM; and under Brig, MR. STAR PITCHER AND MR. PREZ OF HONOR SOCIETY.

The two Mr. Prezes and me.

"What a bunch of bullcrap," Brig said, but he loved it. We all did.

We get along great, only sometimes Brig will say something to get under Candy's skin, like joking about Candy's parents being the Beautiful People in public but killing each other in private. We all know Candy's parents fight, but we don't talk about it. Sometimes Candy blows it off, but once he went for Brig like he wanted to kill him. I thought I was going to have to mop up the blood. I pried them apart. I wouldn't take sides. I never do. Sometimes I say, "You're right, Candy," but another time I'll say, "Brig's got it." Mostly, though, I just lean back and say, "Whatever."

I love that word. You can just . . . say it. Drawl it out. And the moment you do, you can relax. You don't have to choose: Candy or Brig. You don't have to decide if you want cheese pizza or pizza with sausage, if you want to go swimming or play racquetball, if you want to see a movie or rent a video. You don't have to think about anything. You don't have to think about . . . her. You don't have to figure out if what you did was right or wrong. You can just sort of blank your mind and go . . . *whatever*.

– 1 –

Rollo is sitting outside school with his friends, finishing his lunch. It's one of those early December days that are cold, but sunny enough so you can sit on the stone steps and not freeze your ass. The sun on Rollo's face is great. He ignores the off-and-on throbbing in his elbow. He's getting really relaxed. No pressure, no tension, just letting go, getting really, really relaxed.

He takes a bite of his sandwich. It's so perfect sitting with his friends like this. He sees them in his mind like a picture. THREE FRIENDS TOGETHER. The big wide one in the middle, loose-limbed smooth old Candy on one side, and Brig, all wires and springs, on the other side. Sometimes, the best times, like now,

Rollo has this pure, certain feeling that the three of them *belong* together and that they'll always be together.

He leans back on his elbows, then jerks upward. He can't put pressure on his right elbow. Feels like little knives cutting up a steak. From September until Thanksgiving, when football ends, and even after for a while, he always aches and throbs someplace in his body. His ribs are still sore from Brady, that ox from Boonville, butting him. The last game, and Brady sure wanted to smash him, but Brady was the one who went down, with Rollo on top of him and Scipio slipping through with the ball.

Last week, Coach gave them his end-of-the-season speech. "I want you men to stay in shape the rest of the year. We had a decent season, not a great season, but nothing to be ashamed of. We did our best, we gave it our all, that's what counts." He made them hold hands and yell, "We did our best, we gave it our all!"

Then he went around grabbing each player by the shoulder and telling him all his excellent points and how he should work out through the winter and spring and have strong mental thoughts about playing next year. He gave each one a hug and a big slap on the back.

When he came to Rollo, he gave him the slap on the back, but not the hug. "Wingate, you disturb me," Coach said. "You should be better than you are." His face was puckered up: he looked like his teeth hurt. "Something's missing, Wingate. What is it?" Coach tapped Rollo's chest. "A four-letter word, begins with *T,* and a six-letter word, begins with *S.* I'll give you a hint. The four-letter word is *team.*" Coach's face was right up against Rollo's.

Rollo stood straight, his shoulders back, his neck rigid, like a marine in one of those movies where the sergeant is yelling at the recruit, and the recruit is not supposed to show any feelings, only yell out, "Yes, SIR! . . . No, SIR!" Rollo wished he could just tell Coach the truth.

"The six-letter word ends with *T,*" Coach went on. "I'll give you some of the other letters, because this is a tough question. *S. P. Blank. R. Blank. T.*"

Everyone was listening. A lot of the guys were laughing. Coach waited, and Rollo had to say it, feeling like a damn fool. "Team spirit."

"Right! And I don't think you have it."

"Uh, I do," Rollo lied. "I do. Really." He said it to make Coach feel better. It wasn't Coach's fault the way Rollo was. Coach had done everything a coach should do. He'd screamed at Rollo, he'd pushed him, he'd called him names, he'd whacked him across the side of the head, he'd even appealed to him.

But Rollo still lacks team spirit, still doesn't like football. He doesn't know why. He doesn't understand why he's this way, when other kids would give anything to be on the team, in his shoes. Maybe it's the same way he doesn't like clams or listening to his father's music. Matter of taste.

"Let Rollo decide," Candy is saying. "Yes or no, Rollo?"

What's he supposed to decide? He hasn't been listening. "Whatever," he says and shifts on the cement steps, sucking in the fresh cold air. God, he feels happy. Football is over. He is free as a bird. Nobody telling him to do anything. Nobody on his case. Nothing to think about.

"Hey, Rollo," a kid says, coming up the steps. He gives Rollo a big, hero-worshipping smile. "Rollo, man!"

"Yeah, hi," Rollo says. There are always kids around like that, looking at you like you're something special because you're on the team. The kid gives Rollo a kick in the ribs as he passes, like he thinks Rollo is made of stone.

Candy and Brig laugh. "Rollo, man!" Brig says. "That kid's in love with you. You return the feeling?"

"Shut your nasty mouth, Briggers."

"Get off your oversize ass, Wingate, and make me."

They slap hands.

"When do you guys think my brother did it the first time?" Brig says.

"Knowing your big brother, when he was in diapers," Candy says.

"Close. He was thirteen."

"Says who?" Candy sounds cool, but Rollo notices that his freckles get bright. Whatever Candy does, playing basketball or leading an assembly, he makes it look easy, but sometimes those freckles give him away.

"What about you and Arica?" Candy says to Brig.

"What about us? Eat your heart out."

Rollo wonders if it's true, or ... Probably it is. Brig and Arica. Sure. By now ... He watches Denise Dixon crossing the bare, half-frozen lawn. Now, there is something perfect. She's wearing a green sweater, down vest, and black pants. Blond hair, pink cheeks, tiny waist. You just want to put your hands around that waist and squeeze.

Rollo is sure Denise Dixon is the kind of girl you could talk to, and she would listen and make it easy for you to say things. She sits behind him in Mr.

Maddox's class. Sometimes Rollo feels Denise Dixon's breath on the back of his neck and senses her pretty legs behind him, and then everything fades away—Mr. Maddox's voice becomes a faint drone, the classroom is gone, everything is gone, Rollo is gone. . . .

They have never talked. She's one of the smart girls, one of the beautiful, perfect girls you can just look at and think about in private. Sometimes a girl will glance at him in the hall and say, "Hiii, Rollo. How are *yooou*?" But not Denise Dixon. That's okay, because if she did talk to him, what would he say?

"I might go out with her," Candy says, pointing with his chin.

"Who?" Brig asks.

"Denise Dixon."

"You're going out with Denise Dixon?" Brig whistles. "When?"

Candy rubs his chin. "When? When I decide to."

Brig sits back. "You putz."

"Got you that time, Briggers." Candy slaps hands with Rollo.

"You need help, Candrella," Brig says, "serious help. I'm going to have to fix you up."

"The hell you will," Candy says, but he leans forward.

"Yeah, I'm going to do it. I'll ask Arica to recommend someone for a desperate guy. No, wait." Brig's head swivels. "I have a better idea. You should go out with *her*."

They all watch a tall girl crossing the street. She's wearing a long coat, men's work boots, and a gray fedora with a big droopy feather in the brim.

"I'll go out with her if I can keep my eyes closed," Candy says.

They laugh and Brig punches Rollo lazily. "Candy's an amusing cuss," he says.

Valerie Michon clumps up the wide cement walk toward them. They are sprawled out over the steps like it's home and they aren't inviting anyone to enter. They have left a narrow aisle at one end, but as Valerie approaches, Brig shifts and spreads out, so he takes up that space, too.

She stops at the bottom of the steps. "Are you going to move?"

"Why?" Brig spreads out a little bit more.

Rollo and Candy look at each other, smiling.

"I want to go in the building," she says.

"So go."

She walks up the steps, straight up, as if Brig doesn't exist, not trying to get around him or by him, and she steps on his hand, which is in her way, steps right on it with her big, work-booted foot. Brig swears and, quick as lightning, smacks her on the leg.

She jumps like a chicken. She squawks and snatches off her hat as if she's going to beat him up with it. Brig cowers in mock fear, her face goes red, and the three of them are laughing and laughing as she goes into the building.

– 2 –

At the first rumble of thunder, Kara, who's been in the kitchen baking cookies, is out of there and into the front hall closet. "I'm scared I'm scared," she cries. "Rollo, Rollo!"

"It's okay, I'm here," he says, coming in from the living room. "I'm right here, you can come out. Are you coming out?"

"Noooo."

He sits down on the floor near the closet. This is going to take a while. It always does. "Kara . . . are you listening to me?"

There's an acknowledging sob from inside the closet.

"Kara, I have a joke for you."

The windows light up. Thunder rattles every pane in the house, and Rollo's belly jumps. Close strike.

"Are you scared?" **Kara** cries. "Rollo! Are you very scared?"

"Of course not," he lies.

He looks up at the round stained-glass window over the front door, daisies entwined with lilies. There is something soothing about it, something about it that always makes him think of his mother. She would have liked that window, she would have liked this house.

The first time his father brought them here, Kara had shouted, "Nice house! I love it! Nice house, Daddy!" But Rollo, looking into each empty echoing room, had realized with a pang that moving to Highbridge from the city meant leaving behind the place where his mother had lived with them. Everything about Highbridge had seemed strange and lonely until he met Brig and Candy.

"Kara," he says, "are you listening? Here's the joke. Do you know how to catch a special rabbit?"

"What is a special rabbit?"

"Kara, you're supposed to say, *How?*"

"How?"

"Unique up on it."

"Whaaat?"

"*Unique* means 'special.' " He waits. "And it sounds like 'you sneak.' "

"What?"

"Let's try the second part of the joke. Do you know how to catch a tame rabbit? Now you have to say—"

"How?" she cries triumphantly.

"Tame way. Unique up on it."

There is silence from the closet, then Kara says, "Is that a funny joke, Rollo?"

"Not very," he admits. The rumbling in the sky seems to have swung away to the north.

"Rollo. Tell me the story when you were hit by lightning." She pronounces it like three separate words. Light. En. Ing.

"Kara, you always cry when I tell you that. We don't have to talk about it. I'm safe and sound, I'm right here, and I can never be hit again."

"I know, I know! Because lightning doesn't strike two times," she says. "When is the thunder going away?"

"Now. I can hardly hear it anymore. It's raining, that's all. Come on out now." He doesn't want their father to come home from work and find her in the closet. "Come on, honey," he coaxes. "Come out."

The door opens a crack, and Kara appears,

scrunched down, arms wrapped around legs. She duck-walks to him.

"Why are you doing that?" he says.

"I'm being super-safe. Closer to the ground is safer." She sits down and leans her head against his arm. "Tell me about being hit by lightning."

"I've told you so many times, Kara."

"How many times?"

"I don't know. Ten. Twenty. A million."

"A million! That's funny!" She laughs and thumps her head against his shoulder. "That's funnier than rabbit jokes! A million times! I love you, my funny brother, and I love Daddy. And I love your friends, and I love my friends."

"I know, you love everybody."

"Yes," she says with satisfaction.

"Aren't you hungry? I'm starved. Let's go get something to eat. Those cookies smell great."

"I never eat when it's thunder and light. En. Ing. It's a rule. It's a good rule I made up."

"For once, you could break your rule."

"Tell me the story first," she says cannily.

Rollo gives in. "Mom and I were on the porch," he begins.

"You were little."

"Right. I was sitting in her lap—"

"No. You have to say you were little first."

"I was little first."

"No, **Rollo**! Say it right. Say the story right."

"**Is that the** phone I hear?" He puts his hand to his ear. She loves answering the phone.

"No, stupid, it's not even ringing."

"Are you sure? I think Maureen said she wants to eat supper with us. Maybe she's calling."

"Maureen! Oh, no! Now I have to fix up the dining room," Kara moans.

The only time they eat in the dining room is when Maureen, their father's girlfriend, comes for supper, which is practically never, since she thinks they are a bunch of slobs. They aren't *that* bad. It's just that she once caught the three of them eating spaghetti from a common pot, and she's never forgotten it.

"Oh, what a day." Kara clutches her head. "First lightning and now Maureen. I have so many things to think about."

Rollo takes pity on her. "I'm wrong, Kara, I got mixed up. Maureen's not coming today."

"Anyway, you can't answer phones in storms," Kara says, "it's a rule. Don't sit by windows, it's a rule. Don't put on TVs, it's a rule. Outside, stay—"

"All right, enough rules. I got it."

"—low to the ground, it's a rule. Don't sit on—"

"I'm telling you the lightning story," Rollo says. "Do you want me to tell it or not?" Anything is better than listening to Kara going on about her rules. "I was little and there was a storm with thunder and lightning. Mom and I were watching from—"

"You shouldn't have been outside," Kara interrupts. "It's dangerous."

"Mom thought we were safe on the porch."

"We had a big porch then. I remember."

"Right. It was the house Dad and Mom rented for the summer on the lake. You were sleeping, taking a nap. Mom and I were on the porch, sitting in a metal chair—"

"You were just a little teeny three years old."

He nods. "So the lightning hit the ground near us and surged to the porch."

"Surged to the porch!" she moans.

"Kara, it just means it traveled."

"It traveled on its lightning feet! It ran to the porch and it got my little brother and my mommy!" Her face fills.

"Come on, it's only a story. It's all over, it was a long time ago. I'm not going to tell you if you cry."

"I won't! But I can't help it too much. My poor

little Rollie. What did you feel like?" she begs him.

"Poor little Rollie felt like you do when your hands are wet and you touch something electric."

"Zzzzz," she says, grinding her teeth. "Zzzzzzz!"

"Only I felt it all through my body. Zzzzz zzzzz everywhere."

"Ugh!" she cries. "And what about Mommy? You didn't tell me that part again."

"Mom got knocked unconscious for a few minutes. It was worse for her than me, because she was in direct contact with the metal. I was in her lap, so I was mostly protected."

"Yes," Kara says, "it was worse for her. Then what?"

"Well, then she came to, and Dad came home and she told him about it, and he said, 'Oh, my goodness, I'm so upset, I feel so bad, where's my Kara, is she all right?' "

This is the part of the story Kara really likes. "He was worried about me. He was so worried about me."

"But you were safe, taking a nap." Rollo tries to wind up the story quickly. "And it never happened again, and we all got smart and we don't ever sit in metal chairs on porches when there are storms. Let's go fix something for supper."

Suddenly Kara farts. "Oops," she says.

"Kara, that was gross. Remember what Dad told you?"

"I know, I know! I'm supposed to go out of the room, but it just jumped out and surprised me." She giggles. "Excuse me, that was rude. Are you mad? Don't be mad at me."

"I'm not mad at you," he says, holding his nose.

She giggles again and hugs his arm. The storm has really passed by now, and in a few minutes they go into the kitchen and start working on supper together. "I'm a good worker," Kara says, slicing a tomato carefully. "Mrs. Rosten said, 'Kara, you are a good worker. You clean the tables so good. Kara, it's a pleasure to see you, you always have a smile on your face.' " She smiles to show him. "Mrs. Rosten is my social worker. Did you remember that, Rollo?"

"Yes."

"Can I make some tea with sugar?"

"I guess so."

"Oh, good! Thanks!" She puts on the kettle, then stands staring out the rain-smeared window, her thumb in her mouth, her finger absently rubbing her nose. His sister. His big sister, born ten years before him. He had passed her when he was six years old. Ever since, he's been getting older, but Kara has stayed pretty much the same age.

– 3 –

Rollo stares at Sara Hendley—fluffy blond hair, big big blue eyes. She is one of the girls who sometimes says hello to him in the hall.

"She's gonna get all red," Brig predicts.

Candy disagrees. "I've seen her in class, she's cool."

They are in the cafeteria, sitting at their table, the one they staked out for themselves at the beginning of the semester. They are leaning back, sipping sodas, and looking at girls. Behind them, the high windows are streaked with a cold gray rain.

"Red face, big time," Brig says firmly. "Rollo?"

"Uh, maybe she'll twirl her hair," he suggests.

Candy laughs and says he'll go with that. But then Sara Hendley looks up, sees them staring at her, and turns bright red. So Brig wins that round.

It's a game. They choose a girl, then guess what she'll do when she becomes aware of their staring. Sometimes the girl drops something—her napkin, her purse, her fork. Sometimes she gets very animated and starts talking really fast to her friends. Sometimes she tries to pretend she doesn't know they are staring, but they can always tell—she knows. They always get some reaction.

They take turns picking the girl. After Sara Hendley, it's Rollo's turn to pick one. He rubs his elbow where it's sore and glances around the cafeteria. His gaze lingers for a moment on Denise Dixon. No. He squirms a little on his seat. He would never suggest her for the game.

"Well, who?" Brig elbows him. "Don't fall asleep on us."

"Let the big guy think," Candy says.

"Big guy doesn't think," Brig says. "Big guy just goes ugga ugga. He's not that interested in girls, anyway, are you, Rollo?"

"I am," Rollo protests.

"You never get stirred up about anything. If Sara Hendley flashed in front of you, you wouldn't even blink. You'd rub your head and say to yourself, Is it getting hot in here or something?"

They all laugh. Rollo laughs the loudest.

"So who is it?" Candy asks.

"Her." Rollo makes a quick choice, lifting his chin to indicate a tall, rangy girl sitting two tables away from them.

"That dog. That's the best you can do?" Brig complains. He punches Rollo. "We're supposed to pick pretty ones."

They all stare at Valerie Michon.

"She's going to drop her book," Rollo says.

"No, she'll pretend she doesn't notice and talk to that guy sitting next to her," Candy says.

"She's not going to talk to him, she's going to dump her milk on his head," Brig says.

"She's going to start yapping," Candy says. He likes to be right. "She looks like a yapper."

"She was in my AP class last year," Brig says. "I hate girls like her. She argues about every goddamn little thing."

They stare at Valerie Michon, waiting to see which one of them is right. It's a game, just a game, just something to do on a boring, rainy day in December.

Gradually, she becomes aware of them; she looks their way, frowning, sees them staring at her, sees that all three of them are looking at her, just her, pinning her with their eyes. It's always funny watching this happen. Sometimes the girl's head comes up abruptly and she glances at them, then away, then back again, as if she can't quite believe. . . . Sometimes it's just a little side glance that tells her, *Yes, right, someone, no, three someones are staring at you.* . . . And then the red rises in her face or the fork falls or she giggles wildly or . . . whatever.

When Valerie Michon realizes they are staring at her, though, she stares back, just stares right back at them. The game's no fun with her. They should have known. "Remember the way she went up the steps?" Candy says. They all groan. She had come down on Brig's hand as if she was out to break every bone in it, the bitch.

Rollo leans back, thinking about Denise Dixon again. From here, he can see the long straight line of her back, the thick honey-blond braid tied with different-colored yarns. *Lovely thing.* . . . Sometimes he thinks things like that, they just pop into his mind— things he would never say to anyone. *Lovely lovely thing.* . . .

He has completely forgotten Valerie Michon, and then there she is, standing at their table, looking at them, and saying in a voice of utter contempt, "Morons."

– 4 –

"Valerie." Someone touches her on the back, and without thinking she jerks away, reacting as if it were one of those boys.

"Valerie," Mr. Maddox says again, hovering, tall and slightly stooped, over her, "how're you doing? I miss you in class." He pushes up the sleeves of his white sweater with pale, soft hands. Does he know that kids say he's gay? "I don't have anybody to keep me on my toes this year," he says.

"You mean nobody to argue with you!"

She's been told she talks too loud and too much. That just really means she says what's on her mind. Sorry, but if all you can do is utter polite lies, you might as well not live. Just go jump off a cliff and get it over with.

"What are you up to these days, Valerie?" Mr. Maddox says. "Are you working on your art?"

She frowns. "I don't want to talk about that." She doesn't have anything going right now. For some reason, she hasn't been inspired lately.

"What about college—where are you going to apply?"

"I might not go to college."

"Valerie, I don't know if I like that. I don't want to see you throw your talent and ability away."

"Maybe I'll just go to New York City . . . and live and be an artist." How does she get the nerve to call herself an artist? She's an amateur, a beginner, a novice. She wants to take back the words and, at the same time, she wants to shout them out. "Do you really think I have talent?" she can't help asking.

"First prize in the Art Open!"

"School stuff, Paul. I'm not impressed." Is he going to take offense that she used his first name? "I hope, I believe I have talent and—"

"You do, Valerie." He's looking at her with warm eyes.

"That's why I have to . . . I have to *do* something

with it! The whole thing with my hands is so mysterious." The same thing she said to her father last night. Did he understand? He gave her one of his vague, sweet smiles. "When my hands get on the clay, they do things I don't even know are in me. It's as if God gave me something, I mean if you believe in God, which I don't, actually. I do believe in something, a higher power. There has to be something regulating the universe, it can't just be chaos."

She's talking too fast, but he's listening, and she rushes on. "I feel I'm part of whatever this is, something bigger than me—a great universal spirit—and I can't just go off to college and waste my father's money and not do what I'm supposed to do, whatever that is. College, art, talent—it's all tied in together," she finishes. She waves her hands, her heart is pumping, she doesn't know if she said anything that made sense.

"You think if you go to college, you won't be serving your talent?" Mr. Maddox says.

She loves that he puts it all into one simple sentence. She loves that he uses the word *serve*. That he understands. She feels like hugging him, but of course she can't. Her eyes light on his sweater with its intricate knit pattern around the collar and cuffs.

"Fabulous sweater." She knows that will please him. His wife knits all his sweaters.

"My wife made it," he says eagerly. "Talk about talent, Valerie! I want Sandy to go into business. Already one whole room in our apartment is filled just with her patterns and wools. She has so much dedication—"

"Mmm, mmm." Now Valerie remembers that when Mr. Maddox talks about his wife, he is as close to boring as he ever gets. Thank goodness, the bell rings, and she can head upstairs for the art room. It's empty and all hers. She breathes in the quiet, the sharp smell of paints, and the damp acrid smell of clay.

She gets the clay out of the covered tray, sits down on a stool, and starts warming the lump in her hands. Maybe, if something starts happening with it, she'll skip sixth period. Catching a glimpse of herself in the mirror, she straightens her back. Does she look like an artist, someone free and unconventional? She's tall and thin, with pale skin and dark hair. A description that could fit a million people!

She begins working the clay, watching her hands. Are they really an artist's hands? Does she have talent or only cleverness? Her father says everybody has latent talent. She'll never know, though, until she gets out into the real world. Her fingers dig into the clay, and she dreams about living in a little apartment somewhere in Brooklyn. That's where all the artists are now. That's where she can really be herself.

In Highbridge, everyone lives in the same kind of house, drives the same kind of car, goes to the same school, wears the same clothes, and has the same interchangeable parents. Well, actually, there is one exception. As Janice, longtime next-door neighbor and mostly good friend, has said more than once, "Val, your father is *different*."

For starters, he's fat and doesn't have a job. Every other father Valerie knows is trim and in shape, they all jog and do strenuous things at the Racquet Club, and they're all doctors and lawyers and professors at the university in the city. Her father has a workshop in the basement where he spends his days inventing things, like a padded helmet for a baby, so that if the kid climbs out of her crib and falls on her head, she won't get brain-dead.

Once, years ago, a big national company bought one of her father's inventions, something to do with making a little part in a big machine more efficient and cheaper. The company paid her father enough money for them to live on, carefully, for a long time.

Ever since, he has been hoping to come up with something else that will make their fortune.

Last spring, the two of them went to New York City to check out Inventors Expo. Thousands of people in the Javits Center, hundreds of booths and inventions like electric underpants or an electronic hairbrush with a display that told you when you'd brushed your hair enough for maximum health. There'd been at least a dozen versions of steel wool holders and maybe a hundred spaghetti and noodle dippers. And what about the Inter Visuometer or the Polyphase Variable Frequency Inverter? Not even the inventors, standing proudly by their inventions, could make clear what they were for.

Her father had fretted about the noise and the crowds, but Valerie had loved it. "It's incredible, Dad! It's incredible," she kept saying. The people in the street dazzled her—their colors, their shapes, their clothes, their *differentness*. Just walking down Fifth Avenue, she heard at least half a dozen languages. If only she'd had her paints with her—acrylics in bright primary colors were what she wanted to catch the clashing, energetic spirit of the city. It's everything that Highbridge isn't.

She looks at what she's done with the clay. Her hands have worked of their own accord, shaping a head. Prominent eyes, full lips. Mark. "Head of a grut," she says and feels like smacking herself across the mouth. *Grut* is like *spick* or *Polack*, an insult. Even to think it makes her as absurd as everybody else.

She probably is.

An image she doesn't want creeps into her mind: those guys in the lunch room staring at her like she's a . . . thing. A wave of depression hits her. What makes her think she's special? She's no better than anyone else. She's just a small-town girl from a small-town high school. Her head sinks down. She's probably not even that talented. She's probably just a mess, an ordinary mess.

"Rollo!" Arica calls, as he comes out of school.

"Hi." He puts up his hand.

"Come on over!" She and Brig are standing at the top of the steps. Brig is leaning against one of the stone pillars, arms crossed. Arica, facing resolutely away from him, has her books mashed against her chest.

Rollo doesn't want to get too close to whatever is going on there, but Arica reaches for him, almost spilling her books. "We're going to get something to eat," she says. "Come with us."

They start down the hill into town. It's a nearly silent walk. Rollo can never think of small talk, and right now, with Brig so silent, anything he thinks of doesn't seem worth saying. But walking between Arica and Brig, he imagines that he's their guardian . . . guardian angel, maybe. Taking care of them. Maybe he'll get them to make up. They've quarreled before, and it always makes Brig miserable.

A few snowflakes fall. "Maybe we'll get enough for powder," he ventures.

"That would be great!" Arica's enthusiasm is nice. Every now and then she sways against Rollo, as if blown by a little wind. Really, she's so pretty he can hardly look at her.

"Do you cross-country or downhill, Rollo?" she asks.

"Downhill."

"Me too. I love it. Isn't it awful, the middle of December, and we still haven't had a good snowfall?"

He nods. With just a tiny movement of his hand, he could touch her. With a tiny movement of his other hand, he could touch Brig. He's so much bigger than both of them that he could gather them up in his arms . . . and crush them . . . or kiss them. The wind blows. His face feels rough and burning. Stupid thoughts. He's always having stupid thoughts.

They pass the YOU ARE ENTERING THE TOWN OF HIGHBRIDGE, POP. 13,560 sign and go the length of

Seneca Street, past the bank, travel agency, bookstore, restaurant. The old Stoddard Hotel always flies the American flag from the balcony. Here's the tiny movie house that Kara loves, there's the copy shop, and now they're passing his father's office, which is upstairs above the antique store.

"She's talking about breaking up," Brig says suddenly. He jerks his thumb across Rollo at Arica. "She doesn't like me anymore. What do you think of that, Rollo?"

"It's not true," Arica says. "I do, too, like you."

"Doesn't like me," Brig says. "Doesn't like me."

"Stop!" Arica puts her hands over her ears.

"Sorry," Rollo says.

"What are you apologizing for, Rollo?" Arica says.

He doesn't know. He just wishes everyone would be more friendly.

Suddenly Brig pushes Rollo aside and gets next to Arica. He pulls her toward him. "Stay with me, babe," he says in a kind of rough, movie-gangster voice, "or I'll rub ya out."

"That's not funny, Brig."

"Rollo thinks it's funny, don't you, Rollo?"

Rollo grins responsively, feeling stupid again.

Arica pulls free. "Brig, I'm going to say this again,

in front of Rollo, like a witness. All I said to you was that my mother doesn't want me getting too serious. She says—"

"I know what your mother says."

"—I'm too young to be tied to anyone, and you and I—"

"I heard it! Don't tell me that again!"

Arica bites her lip and is silent. They walk across the McDonald's parking lot and into the restaurant. Rollo takes off his jacket and rolls up the sleeves of his shirt. It's hot here; the baskets of plants hanging from the ceiling seem to give off a steamy warmth.

"We can still go out, Brig, we can still be friends," Arica says as they stand in the food line. "I just can't go out with you so much. I can't be exclusive, is all."

"You want to go out with other guys," Brig says. "That's what this is all about. Why don't you admit it? Maybe you want Rollo here. Maybe that's who you want."

"Order me a shake," Arica says and walks away.

"Where're you going?" Brig calls.

She stops briefly. "To wash my hands! I hope, when I come back, Brig, you can be in a better mood."

Rollo and Brig get the food in silence and sit down. "So what do you think?" Rollo says.

Brig is biting the inside of his cheek. "What do I think about what?"

"Will Arica change her mind?"

"How do I know? How do I know anything that goes on in a girl's mind?"

Rollo pours ketchup on his hamburger and looks around for Kara. He spots her swabbing the floor in another aisle. He sees her mouth moving, and he knows exactly what she's saying as she swabs past each booth. "Watch your feet. Watch your feet." She'll say it even if the booth is empty. Sometimes she'll vary it. "Express train coming! Watch your feet!"

When Arica comes back, she hesitates, then sits down next to Brig. She unwraps her straw and puts it into the shake.

"Nice clean hands?" Brig inquires.

Arica smiles tightly.

Nobody says anything for a while. Rollo catches Arica staring at his bare arms. What is she thinking? His arms are hairy, and they seem to him, looking down at them, like enormous, dark sausages. Is she revolted? He checks on Kara again. She's talking to a man sitting alone. Rollo recognizes the sparkling, excited look on her face and hears her voice above all the other voices. He can see only the back of the man's head, but he imagines his startled, annoyed face and half stands. "Kara," he calls.

She looks up. "My brother!" She drops her mop and comes running over. "Rollo!" she says joyously, as if she hasn't seen him for years. She kisses him on the cheek, a loud wet smack. "My darling brother is here! And Mister Brig! This must be my lucky day!" She eyes their food. "You're having a snack. That's great! What's your name?" she says to Arica. "You're pretty!"

Her cap has gotten knocked sideways in the excitement. Rollo pushes it straight. "This is Arica," he says. "Arica, this is my sister. I just wanted to say hello," he says to Kara. "Maybe you better go back to work now."

"Arica, I love you!" Kara bends over and kisses Arica on the cheek and the neck. "Lovely lady Arica!"

Brig laughs. "You're something else, Kara." He likes her.

Arica is looking a little startled. "Did you leave your stuff in the middle of the floor, Kara? Someone might trip over it and hurt themselves."

"Oh, my goodness." Kara looks horrified. She rushes away.

"She's Down's syndrome," Rollo says to Arica.

"I thought it was something like that. Is she always that goofy?"

Rollo dips fries in ketchup. Kara's motor does get sort of revved, but she's not goofy. That's not an accurate way to talk about her. He's disappointed in Arica. If he had a girlfriend and she said something dumb about his sister, what would he do? Dump her or try to improve her attitude?

"Look who's here," Brig says. He's looking over Rollo's shoulder, toward the food line.

Rollo turns. Valerie Michon is in line with a guy he recognizes from around school—Mark Saddler, a senior, one of the kids who comes from Union. A grut.

"That's the girl I told you about who stepped on my hand," Brig says to Arica. He's still staring at Valerie Michon.

"Is that her boyfriend?" Arica asks.

"She's too ugly to have a boyfriend."

"I don't think she's that ugly."

"You wouldn't."

"What does that mean?"

"You girls stick together. You don't even know her."

"I was just giving my opinion, Brig, but I can see you're not interested."

"Oh, I'm interested. I'm always interested in your opinion. And I'm interested in your plan. What is your plan, Arica? First you break up with me, and then you get yourself someone else?"

"I told you, we can still be friends and go out sometimes."

"And I told you, I don't want to be your damn friend."

Rollo tries once more to ease the tension. "You guys ever hear about the grut who picked his nose because he thought he could make it through school by being snotty?"

Arica laughs like she's never heard a grut joke before, but Brig still looks really furious.

– 6 –

They see Valerie Michon in the hall near the art room a day or so later. They are all together. "Look who's here again," Rollo says. Suddenly Brig veers toward her, and Rollo and Candy veer with him. She doesn't see them coming at first; when she does, her face gets this sort of puffy, twitchy look. Funny as hell. They go straight for her, rushing, like a mini-phalanx, like war.

At the last moment, Brig puts out his hands as if he's going to grab her tits. And then, at the last last moment, he veers off, and they sweep by her. Definitely amusing. Rollo and Candy can't stop looking at each other and laughing, but Brig just shrugs. Since the fight with Arica, Brig has not been pleased with anything.

After school, Rollo goes home with Brig. He's complaining about his father, who, he says, has got a new bug in his ear. "He's after me to go to vet school. He says it's not too soon to make up my mind. He says he built up his business and he wants his son to take it over."

"What do you think?" Rollo says.

"No way. No way am I following in Dr. Briggers's tiny footsteps. Not this son."

"Maybe your brother will go to vet school."

Brig coughs dryly. "Forget that. Justin makes my father nervous. You know what my mother told me once? 'Nature didn't favor your brother with as quick a mind as yours, Julian, so your father and I have to give him incentives.' Bribes, she meant. That's how Justin got the Ford, for passing his junior year. And then the Honda, for getting into college."

Rollo nods. It seems like a good deal to him. Brig has been the owner of the Ford since September; in two months, he'll take his road test, and they're all looking forward to it. Rollo and Candy both have licenses, but no cars—Rollo, because his father says he can't afford it, and Candy, because his father says he doesn't want him driving until he's older. What

Candy's father really doesn't want, they've all agreed, is Candy getting into trouble that could make bigger trouble for Senator Candrella.

At Brig's house, they head for the kitchen, and Rollo mixes a power shake, dumping in raw eggs, vanilla, ice cream, and peanut butter. While he mans the blender, Brig hangs from the doorframe: he's trying to lengthen himself, stretch himself taller. An ongoing project.

"Hello, son." Brig's father comes in from the clinic next door. He's wearing a white smock with a stethoscope dangling from the breast pocket. He goes to one of the refrigerators and takes out a brown bag. "Julian," he says.

"What?" Brig says, dropping to the floor.

"I said hello to you. I didn't hear a response. When I speak to you, I expect a response."

Rollo gets a couple of glasses from the cupboard and wishes he could just leave right now. He knows what's coming.

"When I say, 'Hello, son,' the response I expect is 'Hello, Dad.' "

"Okay," Brig says.

Dr. Briggers pours beans into the coffee grinder. " 'Okay, *Dad,*' is the proper mode of response."

"Okay, Dad," Brig says tightly.

"Thank you." Dr. Briggers washes the coffeepot. "What happened in school today?"

"Nothing."

"I believe you had a test in history?"

"Yes."

"What kind of test was it? True, false? Fill in the blanks? Essay?"

"Essay."

"Ahhh. Essay. What was the subject?"

"World War Two."

"Julian. Look at me, please. This is something you'll want to do in the world—look people straight in the eye. What aspect of World War Two did you write about in your essay?"

Brig pours the shake into the glasses. "Paris."

"Why Paris?"

"Mrs. Bardino said we should write about some aspect of the European Theater in World War Two."

"Ahhh. What was your background expertise for writing about Paris?"

"I read a book about the liberation of Paris in 1945. *Paris Is Burning.* You want to know who wrote it? Two guys with French names." Brig is talking fast now. "Was it interesting? Yes. Did I like it? Yes. It was pretty exciting for history. Rollo and I are going into the family room now." He motions to Rollo and they start out of the kitchen.

"One moment, son. You didn't say good-bye."

"Good-bye."

"Good-bye, what?"

"Good-bye, Dad."

Dr. Briggers now looks at Rollo.

One of these days, Rollo is going to say something to Brig about his father, something truthful like, *Your father is a crazed psychotic maniac.* "Good-bye, Dr. Briggers," he says politely. He follows Brig into the family room, takes the chair by the window, and drinks his milk shake in one long, relieved gulp.

Brig paces, punching his fist into his hand. "My father has been taking care of dogs and cats for too long. He thinks the whole world is pets and masters." He flings himself on the floor and begins doing push-ups. ". . . five . . . six . . . seven . . ." Up and down he goes, up and down like a machine.

Rollo lets the thought of doing push-ups drift through his mind. Drift in, drift out. He did enough of that stuff under Coach's prodding. He sinks deeper into the chair, sliding down on his spine. What a good thing it is that nobody can see into his mind. *You are weird, Rollo, let me count the ways.*

There. That's just what he means. Bad enough he sort of likes poetry, but now he's mixing the stuff into his regular thoughts. *How do I love thee? Let me count the ways.* That's from a poem Mr. Maddox read them, which is from a whole bunch of poems called something like *The Portuguese Sonnets.* Elizabeth Barrett Browning was the poet. That name just cracks Rollo up, he doesn't know why. Elizabeth Barrett Browning, who wrote all these love poems for her husband.

"First he was her lover," Mr. Maddox had told them. "Yes, you all find that interesting? Robert Browning was a poet, too, a great poet. Men do write poetry. Does that shock you people? It's one of the grown-up things men do, whether you believe it or not."

Brig says Maddox is a homo. Rollo wonders how that can be if he's married, but Brig says he knows one when he sees one. Rollo likes Mr. Maddox. He's fair. Sometimes he's funny. And sometimes he's a pain in the ass, especially when he gets going on how kids don't appreciate anything except videos and football. "Open your minds. It's not a crime to allow a little real passion and feeling to come through. Release your minds from the grip of the ordinary. Be open, receptive. Receive. Expand!" He always has spit on the corners of his mouth. The poor guys up front have to duck not to get sprayed.

". . . seventy-nine . . . eighty . . ." Brig counts, pumping up and down. He keeps going. He passes one hundred.

"You want your shake?" Rollo says. He could drink another one, easy.

"Hands off. . . . Hundred twenty-five . . . hundred twenty-six . . ." Brig gets to 130 and falls flat. Then he jumps up and stands tall in front of Rollo. "What do you think?"

Rollo looks him over. Is Brig taller than the last time he asked? Rollo doesn't see any difference. "Could be," he says judicially.

"Better be! I hang from that goddamn bar fifteen minutes every morning." Brig takes a long drink of his shake. "I'll tell you something, Rollo, I'm not going through life this size. This is not acceptable. Shorter than Candy, shorter than you, shorter than my father, shorter than my goddamn brother. I might as well go into a circus and be a freak." He drinks and paces. "I'm doing something new called visualizing."

"Visual what?"

"Visualizing. Candy gave me the article about it. He found it in one of his mother's magazines. You think about what you want, you visualize it, you put it in your mind, you concentrate on it, and it happens. The idea is for mind and body to work together. Mind visualizes me getting taller, and body does the work. Crackpot idea, isn't it?"

"It could happen," Rollo says. "You're probably still growing."

"What do you mean, probably?"

"I mean, you are."

"Why don't you say what you mean the first time?"

Rollo shrugs and licks out the inside of his glass. Does Brig realize he can be just like his father sometimes?

The phone rings. Brig punches the SPEAKER button. "Briggers residence."

"I want to speak to Julian Briggers," a girl's voice says.

"This is Julian Briggers. Who's calling?"

"Valerie Michon." Her voice is loud in the room. "I have something to say to you."

Brig puts his index finger to the receiver. Bang! Bang! he mouths to Rollo.

"Keep away from me. Keep your hands away from me. Just stay away."

"Hey!" Brig says. "What do you mean, calling up and yelling at me?"

"I am not yelling."

"No? You're going to bust my eardrum like you busted my hand when you stepped on it."

"You refused to move. What was I supposed to do? You know, you're not just rude, you're *crude*. The way you came at me in the hall—"

"I feel sorry for you, if you can't even take a joke."

There is a moment's silence. Then she says, "I understand you go out with Arica Hamilton. That's who I feel sorry for. I pity her."

"Save your pity for yourself, bitch." Brig punches the button and cuts her off. "Do you believe the nerve, to bring Arica in?" He's pacing again. "I talked to her last night. Did I tell you? We talked for an hour, but it was all the same thing, anyway. Her mother says this, her mother says that." He goes to the window and pulls aside the curtain. "I hate that girl," he says with quiet vehemence.

"Arica?" Rollo says, startled.

Brig turns and looks at him. "No, you idiot. Valerie Michon."

– 7 –

When Valerie enters the empty cafeteria, Mark doesn't look up. He is sitting on one of the benches at the back of the room, hands clasped behind his head, eyes fixed on the ceiling. She sits down next to him and waits. "Hi," she says after a moment.

He pushes his glasses up on his nose. "Oh, hi." As if he's just noticed she's there. He is wearing his usual combo of good-fitting jeans, shirt out, and motorcycle boots. He looks at his watch, which he keeps on a long key chain. "You're late."

"Big five minutes," she says, wishing he were less cute. She wants to be businesslike about this tutoring, but she's really attracted to him. When she and Janice were talking on the phone last night, Janice commented that Mark looked like a younger version of Indiana Jones. Now, Valerie sees that it's true— the same wire-rimmed glasses, the same sort of lean, homely-sexy face.

"If I'm five minutes late for my job," he says, "I get docked a quarter of an hour."

"That's not fair!"

"Who said it was?" His expression makes her feel naïve and inexperienced. "Who said anything is fair?" Behind his glasses, his eyes look wet and tired. He's a part-time security guard at a warehouse four nights a week and holds down another job over the weekend. Valerie thinks it's probably illegal for him to work so many hours while he's still in high school.

"Did you work last night?" she asks after a moment.

"Sure did. What'd you do?"

She frowns. What can she say? *Sketched for an hour. Made a phone call to a nasty boy. Had a headache afterward. Made supper for me and Dad, listened to Janice complain about her clothing allowance, got into the spirit and complained about mine. . . .*

Boo-hoo! What a hard life! What if she told him there are times she wishes that she lived in Union, wishes she were a grut? Not that she wants to be poor, no; it's just that it's so ordinary to be her,

Valerie Michon of 50 Academy Street, Highbridge. At least people in Union have *real* problems.

"Anything special you want to work on today?" she asks.

He opens his notebook and takes out a sheet of paper. "A comp I wrote for Mrs. Parryman. I thought you could go over it for me."

"With you," she corrects. She bends over the paper, but she is aware of his watching her. With the eyes of a student? Or a friend . . . or a male? It seems as if their relationship is a confusing mixture of all three.

Sometimes he is almost humbly grateful for her help, and that is nice, and embarrassing, too. She always wants to say, No no, tutoring is something *I* need to do, to contribute. Then sometimes he takes off his glasses and looks at her with those deep brown eyes, and she gets distracted and starts wondering about things that have *nothing* to do with learning. And other times, they get in a certain mood and just joke around, like friends, and that is really nice.

And sometimes he annoys her. He'll do petty things, like he did today, catching her out for being five minutes late. That's when she wonders if he resents her, resents that she lives in Highbridge, that she knows things he doesn't. But what does she really know, except stuff anyone can learn in school—spelling, grammar, things that have nothing to do with life. He's the one who has the real knowledge: he's worked since he was eleven years old.

"Done yet?" He smooths his small bristly mustache, smiling a little, as if he knows she hasn't gone beyond the first sentence.

"In a moment," she says briskly. It's a short composition, not elaborated, not on a very sophisticated level. A lot of errors, too. Disappointing. She's been tutoring him since the beginning of October. It's already mid-December. In more than two months, you'd think—

Stop, she tells herself. What do you want from him, Harvard-quality work? Yes, probably. He's smart and he's tough, and she has got herself involved in wanting him to succeed. She sits for a minute, collecting her thoughts. "What was the assignment, exactly?" she asks.

He produces a small spiral notebook from his shirt pocket and reads, "Two-page essay about life and family." He always has the notebook and two pens neatly lined up in that pocket, as if he's already an engineer.

She glances at the paper again. "Aside from spelling and stuff, which we'll go over, this is basically okay. It's pretty interesting, but it could be better. I have some suggestions."

He takes a pen and waits.

There is something about the way he does this that gets to her—something so patient and hopeful in his face that she almost wants to cry. Instead, she makes her voice as dry as possible. "I think what you intended, Mark, was to contrast the towns of Union and Highbridge. You began doing it, but you didn't carry through. You didn't give any details to substantiate your point of view."

"What details? Everybody knows the difference between Union and Highbridge. All you Highbridge folks have three-car garages, giant fireplaces, and at least two Mercedes-Benzes."

"Saddler, that's ridiculous."

"Looks that way from where I sit."

"Okay, we won't argue about it. Those are your details about Highbridge. What about Union?"

"There's nothing to say about Union."

"Of course there is."

"Do you know Union, Valerie?"

"I've driven through it with my father on the way to the interstate."

"There you go. That's it. Everyone drives through Union on the way to the interstate. That says it all."

"There's got to be something else."

He leans back again, hands clasped behind his head. "Sure there is. Dumpy houses. Biggest store in town is the Salvation Army Thrift Shop. The most action is at Bob's Off-Brand Gas Station. Best restaurant, Pete's Pig-out Pizza. Come on, Valerie, you know Union, it's nothing, the people who live there are nothing, and it's nothing anyone wants to read about."

"I can't believe the things you say. They're totally absurd! You're more prejudiced than anyone in Highbridge."

"You think so?" he says mildly, but there's a flash in his eye.

"Look, the point is, you've got to put the details in the essay. All that stuff will make an excellent contrast to your observations about Highbridge."

"Ahh, yes, the fine details of Union, an excellent contrast to my profound observations . . ."

Okay, so she had sounded stuffy. "Write it down," she orders. "You know you can do better than this. Some of your vocabulary is so lazy, like using 'bummed-out.' And you've got run-on sentences, plus spelling errors."

He sucks on the end of his pen. "Is this stuff going to help me get into college?"

"It's going to help, yes. I wouldn't be doing this, spending all this time, if I didn't think so."

"All this time," he repeats. "Your valuable time."

A little heat comes up into her neck. Why is there always this barrier she can't get past with him? Why does he put this wall up between them? All she wants is to be his friend. Doesn't he get it! What sort of person is he behind those flip remarks—is he genuine? You can't tell about some people. Faces can be so deceptive, and maybe guys' faces, especially, because she's always distracted by how their hair grows a certain way or their eyes have a particular light.

The thought of those three jerks swims into her mind. Perfect examples of the adorable face–cruddy attitude syndrome. Briggers has a great body and fantastic hair. Candrella is sort of an All-American type. He could step into an ad and model shirts or jeans. And the other one, the football one—she's forgotten his name, but the one who's fat and dumb—even he isn't so bad to look at. With his round eyes and round mouth and fair hair cut straight across his forehead, he looks like a cute boy doll.

She glances at Mark again, at his eyes, hidden

now behind his wire rims, and wishes, not for the first time, that she knew what really went on in his mind.

"What are you looking so serious about?" he says.

"Just thinking about your sentence structure."

– 8 –

The day it finally snows in earnest, Kara is so excited she can hardly sit still at supper. "I'm going sledding," she says, bouncing in her chair. "It's snowing and blowing and the cat has snow on his whiskers. Rollo, will you go sledding with me?"

"Maybe," he says, reaching for another slice of pizza.

"Rollo, 'maybe' means 'yes.' Did you know that? The cat has snow on his whiskers, that's the joke." She has her face tipped to the side, her eyes opened wide. "I want to go sledding in the cat-whisker snow. Daddy, did you hear me?"

"I heard you, honey. Quiet down now. Let's finish up. Maureen's coming over later."

Rollo glances across the table at his father. It still comes as a surprise to him that his father has a girlfriend. To be brutally truthful, his father is overweight, has a pot belly and round shoulders. His teeth are yellow, too. Do he and Maureen . . . ?

"Maureen's coming over?" Kara says. "Uh oh, this is a mess!" And when Rollo laughs, she repeats it, rolling her eyes, making a nutty face. She knows she's being cute. Just then the phone rings. "It's Maureen," Kara screeches, hoping for another laugh. "Get it, Rollie."

It's not Maureen, it's Brig, who says he has to talk to Rollo and he's coming right over. He doesn't even say good-bye, just hangs up. What's that all about? Arica, probably. Which means Brig won't want to talk in the house, because Kara doesn't know the meaning of the word *privacy*.

"I'm going outside to wait for Brig," he tells his father. "We're probably going for a walk or something."

"Okay," his father says, and, ever the efficient accountant, he adds, "You might as well start shoveling the walk while you wait."

The wet, heavy snow packs into cubes with each shovelful, and the wind blows into Rollo's face. He heats up and tears off his jacket. He has shoveled out to the street and is doing the sidewalk when Brig pulls up. The top of his car is covered with a fat pancake of snow. He rolls down the window and waves Rollo over.

"How come you're driving?" Rollo says, leaving the shovel in a snowbank.

"Because I feel like it."

"What'd your father say?"

"He's at a convention in Texas. Come on, get in!"

"What about your mother? She know you got the car?" Rollo slides into the front seat.

"She's out with friends tonight. Any more questions?"

"You want me to drive?"

"No! Guess what Arica told me—she's going to break up with me."

"I know that. She said that already."

"No, you don't know that!" Brig hits the steering wheel. "She'd changed her mind. I got her to change her mind. Yesterday I talked her out of it." He pulls away from the curb, and the tires spin in the snow. "Then she calls me back tonight and says never mind what she said before."

"Maybe she'll change her mind again."

The car lurches ahead. "If I just didn't have to see her every day in school."

"Winter vacation is coming," Rollo says, trying to be helpful. "A few more days, then you won't have to see her for a long time."

"You don't understand anything." Brig groans and steps on the gas. The headlights barely penetrate the falling curtain of snow.

They drive up the hill, past the school, past the cluster of houses on Birch Hill, and out of Highbridge. Brig is talking about Arica again, his voice choked, saying all the things he's said before: how he feels like crap and how it's Arica's fault he feels this way.

Rollo shifts around. He wants to tell Brig something, maybe to take it easy, maybe just what he'd thought that day in the restaurant when Arica made her dumb remark about Kara. *She's pretty, Brig, but don't get all wiped out over her. There are plenty of other girls around. . . .*

"Where are we going?" he asks, after a while.

"I don't know. . . . How does grut hunting sound?"

It sounds tough and funny, like something someone would say in a movie.

They take the back road over by Union Falls, a winding road of sudden curves that pitches steeply down into the valley. Brig is a good driver; probably they won't be stopped by a cop, but Rollo wipes the side window dry and keeps an eye out, anyway. Banks of snow line the shoulders. The roadbed is covered by a thick blanket of wet snow, and the back of the car is torquing all over the place.

"Want me to slow down," Brig says, not slowing down.

"Go," Rollo says. He loves the speed, loves the way Brig lets the car hurtle down into the valley on the snow-clogged road.

Suddenly there's a gleam of green-gold in midair, and a deer leaps toward them, leaps through the falling snow like a dream. Brig jerks the wheel, and the car slides sideways across the road into a snowbank. They sit for a moment, looking at each other. The deer is gone, swallowed by snow and trees. "He could have totaled the car," Brig says. "He could have killed us."

"Killed us!" Rollo says. He starts laughing with relief and excitement.

They're both laughing as they push the car out of the snowbank. They talk about the deer—how big it was, how much it weighed. "A hundred fifty pounds," Brig says solemnly, "maybe two hundred."

Two hundred pounds of hooves and bones and forward energy that could have smashed them to bits.

"But here we are!" Rollo says triumphantly. They're still laughing as they roll into Union. The main street is nearly deserted. Wreaths are strung around the light poles, and almost every house has blinking candles in the window and a Santa Claus with elves or deer on the roof. Brig drives up one street, down another. The plows haven't been through some of the streets yet.

"How many people do you think live in this town?" Brig says.

"Not many."

"Right, and they're all related, which is why they're all morons. Do we know anybody that lives here?"

Rollo laughs. "You kidding?"

"That guy we saw Valerie Michon with."

"We don't know him."

"He looked grutty!"

"True."

"We could go over to his house and pay him a visit."

"Why?"

"Because I feel like doing something." Brig's voice is tense again. "I just freaking feel like doing something. What's his name?"

"Who?"

"The grut! The one that was with Michon."

"Saddler or something."

"Right, that's it. Mark Saddler. I wonder where he lives."

"We could check the phone book," Rollo says.

Brig jams on the brakes. Across the street is a gas station with an outside phone booth. They get out of the car. The door of the booth is half off, and someone has tried to rip the phone book off its metal chain. Brig thumbs through what's left of the book. "Got it," he says after a minute or two. "There's a Saddler on Elm Street."

They drive around looking for Elm Street. After they go by School Street for the third time, Brig rolls down the window and calls to a girl coming out of a pizza place, "Where's Elm Street?"

She stares into the car. She's holding a stack of white pizza boxes, her chin resting on top. "Over that way." Her lips are outlined in bright pink.

"You going to eat all those pizzas yourself?" Rollo suddenly says. He's getting hungry again. Besides, he likes the way she has those bright neon-pink lips, and he wants to say something to her.

She gives him a nice little smile. "Don't worry about it, sweetie. I've got friends as big as you to help me out. Take your first right," she says to Brig, "go down two blocks, hang a left at the light. Nice car. Whose is it?"

"Mine."

"Honest to God?"

"Two more better than this at home."

"Liar," she says.

"I swear."

"Where's home?"

"Highbridge."

"Oh, that follows."

Her directions are good. The house on Elm Street is painted green, with a square front porch. Santa Claus and three reindeer outlined in red lights are running across the roof.

"What do you think?" Brig says, parking behind another car at the curb.

"Looks okay to me," Rollo says.

"What do you mean it looks okay? You think we're buying the place?"

"I don't know what we're doing."

Brig laughs. "Me either. Let's find out."

"Find out what?"

"If he lives here."

"Then what?"

"I don't know. Didn't you ever hear of improvisation?"

They sit in the car, looking at the house. There are lights on everywhere and they can faintly hear music. Rollo feels a little nervous and clears his throat a few times. "What if it's the wrong house?"

"What are you whispering for?"

Rollo digs his hands into his pockets. "We don't even know this guy, Brig. It's crazy."

"That's the way I feel, crazy."

The front door of the house opens, and a man wearing a green jacket and carrying a gym bag comes down the walk. As he gets closer, they see it's Mark Saddler, and Brig rolls down his window. "Mark," he calls.

Mark Saddler pushes up the nosepiece of his wire-rimmed glasses and bends down to look into the car. "What's up?"

"Where's your girlfriend?"

"What are you talking about?"

"You want to watch out for her," Brig says. "Valerie Michon. She's unnatural."

"What?"

"You know the type, she's like a guy in disguise."

"What do you want? I'm on my way to work, I don't have time for this bullshit." He looks at them. He doesn't say anything else. He just looks, and there is something menacing in the way he does that, in the way he half crouches outside the car, his eyes directly on them, not saying anything, just looking at them as if he's permanently fixing a picture of them in his mind.

Rollo, sitting next to Brig, is not quite breathing. Not holding his breath, either. It's more like his breath is suspended, or maybe it's like being in a dream. No, more like watching the dream. The same as watching a movie. You're waiting for something to happen. You're in suspense. You're interested, absorbed. You're noticing things. You're noticing how Brig's fingers do a little drumbeat on the steering wheel. How, under his bulky jacket, Mark Saddler is in great shape. How your feet on the car floor are pointing in two different directions.

You notice things and you hear things, and you're there . . . but you're not quite there. You're not scared and you're not nervous and you're not belligerent, you're just . . . waiting. You're just there, watching the movie and waiting for the next thing to happen. And it's all interesting and a little thrilling.

"Why don't you just get out of here, Highbridge boys?" Mark Saddler says. "Get the fuck out. You don't belong here."

"Hey!" Brig says. "This is a free country."

Saddler straightens, walks to the car ahead of

them, and reaches into the front seat. Rollo leans forward, his forehead touching the cold windshield. Is Saddler going to come out with a gun in his hand? The slam of Saddler's car door is like a pistol shot.

Saddler starts cleaning the snow off his windshield with a plastic ice breaker. He cleans the window thoroughly, then does the side windows. He goes around to the back of the car and cleans off that window. He doesn't look at them. When he's done, he gets in the car and starts the motor. A cloud of exhaust puffs into the snowy air.

Brig starts his car, too, and turns on the headlights, but neither car pulls away from the curb.

"What are we doing?" Rollo says.

Brig shrugs. "Let him go first."

They sit there for maybe ten minutes, until Brig gets tired of it. "Oh, screw it." He pulls away, skidding his car close to Saddler's as he passes.

Rollo sees Mark's startled face. "You see that," he says to Brig, and then they're both laughing again, and it's just like those moments after the deer almost hit them. They start laughing and they can hardly stop.

– 9 –

"You know what she did now?" Brig says, meeting Rollo near the gym between classes.

"Who, Arica?"

"She walked by me without even saying hello."

"Maybe she didn't see you," Rollo suggests.

"She saw me! That's it, I'm through with her." But that night he phones Rollo and asks him to call Arica and talk to her. "Tell her to come back with me—"

"Brig—"

"She likes you, she thinks you have a nice way of talking. She'll listen to you."

"I won't know what to say."

"I just told you. First you start by saying something

good about me, then you get across to her that she's making me feel lousy."

"Brig—"

"I'm going to hang up. Call her right now," Brig says.

Rollo sits in the hall on the steps for a while before he punches Arica's number. As he listens to the phone ringing in her house, he remembers her calling Kara goofy, and he thinks, since he's actually calling a girl, why her? Why not Denise Dixon? The phone rings again. Does Arica remember what Brig said that day they were all together? *You want Rollo? Is that who you want?*

What if she's been thinking about him? What if she really wants to break up with Brig so she can have *him*? Suppose she gets all excited when she hears his voice. *Rollo, I'm coming over.* He wouldn't have to do anything. He wouldn't have to say anything. He could just wait, and she would come over, and they would go up to his room and lie down on the bed together and—

"Hello?" a high voice says. It's a kid who can't pronounce his *l*'s. "Hewwo?"

"I want to talk to Arica," Rollo says.

"This is Brian. Arica's not here."

"Who is this?" Rollo says.

"Brian. I towd you already. Who is this?"

"Rollo."

"Oh. Arica's at, she's with her girwfriend. Do you want Mommy?"

"No." He hangs up.

Almost instantly the phone rings. "Rollo," Brig says, "how come you didn't call me back?"

"I just hung up."

"So what did she say?"

"I didn't talk to her."

"What do you mean, you didn't talk to her?"

"She was out. Her brother, I guess it was her brother, answered the phone."

"Brian? You talked to Brian? He's the one who told you Arica was out? What'd he say, that she was at her girlfriend's house?"

"Something like that."

"He always says that. You should have said, *Brian, go get Arica!* She was probably right there, watching TV or something. I bet you anything she was in the house. Call her again."

"Again?" Rollo says.

"Yeah. Call her and then call me."

"Okay."

"You're going to do it?"

"Yeah."

"When?"

"Pretty soon."

"You won't forget?"

"I won't," Rollo says. But he does.

– 10 –

Saturday morning, Rollo labors around the track at the Racquet Club. Candy, high-stepping, passes him and taunts, "Puff, puff, puff." Rollo runs twenty laps and cuts out. He could have gone around another dozen laps, but it's too boring. He finds Brig in the weight room. Candy joins them after a while, and the three of them sit around until their racquetball court is open. Then they play cutthroat, two-on-one, switching partners after each game. They play hard for a couple of hours.

Afterward, standing in the showers, Brig analyzes their games and instructs Rollo about his mistakes. "There's such a thing as hitting too hard. You can't hit the ball and not think about the next shot."

Rollo turns off the shower. Okay, he powers the ball, but that's what he has going for him—power and muscle. He loves to let go and smash the ball. He loves the sound of the ball smacking against the racket. He isn't swift and showy like Brig, who likes to run up the walls and kill every ball, and he isn't a precision player like Candy.

"This is a game of strategy, not strength."

"I got strategy," Rollo says.

"Where, in your ass? You see the ball and your muscles start popping and, *pow,* you send it to kingdom come. That's why we lost that third game to Candy." Brig punctuates his words with snaps of the towel. "All you did was set Candy up. You kept sending the ball right back to him."

"Hey, that was my superior playing that won that game," Candy says. He's in front of the mirror, towel knotted at his waist, blow-drying his hair.

Brig zips up his pants. "Why didn't you call me back last night, Rollo? I was waiting."

"Last night?" Rollo dives into his locker for his shirt. "I didn't talk to her," he mumbles.

"Who?" Candy says.

"You didn't talk to Arica?" Brig says.

Rollo shakes his head. "I'll do it, I'll call her today, you can count on it. Just remind me—"

"I'm not reminding you of anything!" Brig's face twitches, and he walks away toward the washroom.

Rollo looks at Candy. "He wanted me to call Arica for him."

"He's really cut up over her. He got too involved. I feel sorry for him. Don't say anything to him now, but I'm going out with Vera Mullin next week."

"Who?"

"Vera Mullin. Don't you know her? Black hair, blue eyes, she's in eighth grade."

"Eighth grade." Rollo rolls his eyes. "You asked her?"

Candy grins. "She asked me."

A group of men walk in and noisily get their gym bags out of their lockers and walk out again.

"You know how I started going with Arica?" Brig says, coming back from the washroom. "She was hanging around my locker. She was giving me the eye. She was saying cute things." He drops down on a bench. "What am I talking about her for? I don't want to talk about her. It's all over." He punches his leg, and he's crying.

Rollo has never seen Brig cry. It's terrible. Brig is making these hoarse, choking sounds, and Rollo can hardly stand it. He pats his friend's shoulder over and over. "I'm sorry, Brig. I'm really sorry. I should have called her. Brig, I'll do it."

"Forget it, I said. I don't care."

"That's the way," Candy says, hovering over Brig, too. "Just forget her. What do you care about her?"

"I don't. I don't care about her."

"Good. You can get another girl."

"Right," Rollo says. "There's lots of other girls,"

"They're like fish in the ocean," Candy says. "Brig just has to drop in his line."

Brig slaps at Candy halfheartedly. "What do you know about it, Candrella? You ever have a girl-friend?"

"Plenty."

"You did?" Rollo says. "When was that?"

"When was that?" Candy mocks, sitting down next to Brig. "You think you know everything about me?"

Rollo lets his mouth drop open and shakes his head like a rube. He's playing dumb, doing it for Brig, to cheer him up. And it seems to be working. Brig is almost smiling.

They sit on the benches facing each other, their knees banged in together, and talk about how many years they've been friends and all the things they've done together. They talk about the other night, how crazy it was the way Brig and Rollo drove down into Union, and the way they faced off with Mark Saddler.

Candy brings up the time he and Rollo broke into the guardhouse near the quarry. And after that they go over the famous night when they all sneaked out of their houses at midnight. "We stayed out until two in the morning," Rollo says.

"No, it was three o'clock," Brig says.

"That was great, that was really great," Rollo says.

"Don't laugh, you guys," Candy says, "I know what I'm going to say is corny, but you know what I'm thinking sitting here listening to all this?" He looks from one to the other of them. "I'm thinking how our friendship is more important than any girl."

Rollo's eyes get damp. He gets his arms around Brig and Candy and sort of hugs them. Then they're all hugging, and their faces are close. Close enough to kiss, Rollo thinks. A weird thought, but maybe Candy has the same weird thought, because suddenly he pounds Rollo on the leg, really pounds him hard, and says, "Hey, cream puff! Hey, you big cream puff!" And they all laugh and break apart.

"Morning," Rollo says. Kara's at the table already, and his father is standing at the counter, looking at the newspaper and drinking coffee. "Oversleep?" his father asks.

"Yeah." Rollo sits down, yawning, and pulls over the corn flakes box. Kara has overfilled her cereal bowl, and milk slops over the sides.

"Slurp it up," Rollo says.

"Not good manners!" She's wearing her pj's and a yellow-striped wool hat.

"You going to work that way? Is that the new uniform?"

"Oh, you joker brother."

Rollo studies the corn flakes box. He has them

every morning. "Do we have any waffles?" No one answers. He pours corn flakes into his bowl.

"What time is it?" his father says, handing Rollo the paper. "Kara?"

She pulls up her pajama sleeve and checks her watch. "Seven-ten. You go to work at seven-fifteen." She stares at the digital dial. "Now it's seven-eleven."

Mr. Wingate bends down and kisses her. "You two have a good day. I'm off now."

" 'Bye," Rollo mumbles, looking at the sports page.

"Daddy, don't go yet," Kara calls, studying her watch. "It's only seven-thirteen."

"Don't worry about it, scout," Rollo says, "it's going to be seven-fifteen any minute now."

It's an ordinary morning, and as usual he meets Candy and Brig on the corner of Locust Street, and they walk through town and up the hill to school together, talking and throwing snowballs at every STOP sign.

It's still an ordinary day when Rollo enters his homeroom. Mrs. Schwartz takes attendance; the principal is on the P.A.

"Good morning, Highbridge-Union students. In three days, our winter vacation starts. I know a lot of you have big plans and are eager to get them under way, but I want to emphasize that these days are still regular working school days. I also want to emphasize that this morning's assembly is for the entire school. Mr. Asquith and the Drama Club have worked hard for many months on this modern interpretation of Charles Dickens's famous play *A Christmas Carol*. Let's reward them with complete attention. Assembly will proceed through fourth period. Those of you who have fourth lunch will just have to go hungry today. No, no, no, only joking, you'll be allowed five minutes extra to buy your lunch and bring it to your next class. . . ."

Later, Brig, Candy, and Rollo each come to the assembly with his own class, but they find one another and go to the back of the auditorium. Coach notices them. "You guys. Do you belong here?"

"Sitting down right now, Coach," Rollo says quickly. Coach nods and turns to some other kids.

Teachers are pacing up and down the aisles. The orchestra is tuning up. Kids are calling to each other. Still an ordinary day. Then Brig sees Arica sitting down front with some other girls, and he motions to Rollo. "Look at her." Up to this moment, he hasn't even mentioned her once. Now his face seems to heat up, his lips thin. He leans forward tensely.

"Brig . . ." Candy says. He looks at Rollo, who digs

in his pocket and finds half a candy bar. He breaks it into pieces and shares it out. Maybe food will make Brig feel better.

The orchestra finally gets going and plays a medley of Christmas carols. Brig is still sitting forward in that tense way, staring toward Arica. The lights go off, the curtain rises, and the play starts.

Candy whispers to Rollo, "Tiny Tim, Scrooge, the Ghost of Christmas Past, blah blah blah."

"You said it." Rollo yawns. At least Denise Dixon is in the play, and the modern clothes make it a little different. Still, his attention wanders, and he's at least half-asleep when Brig elbows him and nods toward one of the EXIT doors, where a girl is leaving the auditorium.

"Michon," Brig says, almost to himself.

He slides out of his seat.

− 12 −

The hall is empty. The three of them stand still for a moment, then Brig walks quickly toward the stairs. Rollo and Candy follow. When they turn the corner, they hear footsteps on the stairs.

"Let's get her," Brig says, and they run up the stairs. They run up the stairs quickly and quietly.

Or maybe Brig doesn't say anything. Maybe Rollo only thinks he hears Brig say that. Maybe it goes like this: They hear footsteps on the stairs, and no one says anything, but they run up the stairs, anyway. They run up the stairs after her. They are fast, they are quiet. They are taking the stairs two at a time. They are running up the stairs quickly and quietly.

On the second-floor landing, they listen, and they

hear the footsteps still going up. Going up to the third floor. They follow. They go up after the footsteps. After Valerie Michon's footsteps. They don't talk about it, they just do it.

It's a game. Fun. They glance at each other, and they take the stairs swiftly, grinning. It's a game, and then, too, it's like a dream. Rollo feels something dreamlike in the way he is running up the stairs, running after Brig so smoothly, so swiftly, and the way Candy is running after him, and the way they are all running up the stairs after the footsteps.

Maybe there is nobody there, Rollo thinks. Just for a moment he thinks that—nobody there, no body, no person, no Valerie Michon. Nobody, just the footsteps leading them on.

Then they are on the third floor and they see her.

Her back is turned to them. She is at the end of the corridor in front of the window that looks out over the woods behind the school.

She doesn't seem aware of them. She's leaning forward, her hands on the windowsill, looking out.

She's like a shadow against the window, like cardboard, a dark cutout against the wintry white light flooding in from outside.

They trot toward her. They are not so quiet now.

She turns and looks at them. She says, "What do

you want?" Her eyes flicker one way, then the other.

She starts to move around them and Brig grabs her. And then they all grab her. They just do it, all together. It happens fast, so fast. It's like reading each other's minds. *Let's get her.* Did Brig say it? They don't say anything now, they just grab her, and you can't tell who does what, whose hands are where.

"Stop! Quit! Oh, damn, no . . . oh . . . oh . . . stop. . . ."

Rollo hears panting. Maybe it's himself. He hears grunts, and he's aware of his hot breath. His face and hands are burning, and his hands are on Valerie: he has some part of her in his hand, some soft flesh, some thrilling part of her.

She's twisting around, trying to get away, trying to get free, but they have her.

Rollo's sweating and grinning. He can feel the grin stretched across his face, and he remembers slipping and sliding down the winding road into Union, the car skidding through the snow . . . dangerous, thrilling. . . . You know you should stop but you keep going, you don't want to stop, you just want that thrill . . . that thrill. . . .

Valerie is flailing and yelling. She wrenches free, her arms swing wildly, and she stumbles and crashes to her knees. Then Brig is trying to straddle her, trying to get on her back, and she's jerking around frantically.

A bell rings and it shrills into Rollo's brain.

He blinks and stumbles back, breathing hard.

Candy pulls at Brig.

Valerie is up on one knee. Her hair is down around her face.

They leave. They walk down the hall, tucking in their shirts.

– 13 –

The auditorium is still dark. The play is still going on. The same characters that were onstage when they left are still onstage, sitting around the laden table: Tiny Tim, Scrooge, the "baby" in the high chair. . . .

Rollo moves quietly toward his seat. He tiptoes, lifting one foot at a time, the way you do when you're entering a room full of people, and you're trying not to disturb anyone. You pick up each foot carefully, put down each foot carefully, and carefully lower yourself into your seat, hoping the floor won't squeak, the seat won't creak.

He sits and looks up at the stage. Denise Dixon is there, her head tilted to one side. Any moment now Tiny Tim will say, God bless us all. . . . Rollo stares at Denise Dixon, and for a moment everything blurs. Nothing is distinct. The stage and everyone on it, the auditorium and everyone in it, collapse into a smear of sound and light. He looks at his friends. Brig is leaning back, legs out, arms crossed over his chest. He catches Rollo's eye and nods soberly. Candy seems absorbed in the play, bent forward, chin in hand.

Rollo's heart slows down, his breath is quiet. He watches the stage.

From the corner of his eye, he sees a door open on the other side of the room. A bar of light appears. Someone leans into the auditorium, someone else rises. All the way across the dark room, Rollo senses whispers, ripples of movement. The door closes again.

"God bless us all!" Tiny Tim cries.

A moment later, a hand taps Rollo on the shoulder. Mr. Maddox's tall and slightly bent form is standing over him. "Come with me," he whispers. He taps Brig on the shoulder, then Candy. The audience is clapping. The three of them follow Mr. Maddox into the hall and down the corridor.

"Where are we going?" Rollo says.

Mr. Maddox glances at him. "Principal's office."

It's not much of a walk, just over the bridge into

the addition, down three steps, and around the corner, but it seems long, because no one says anything after that. Brig whistles quietly. The only other sound is the muted thump of their feet on the wooden floor.

In the outer office, the secretaries look up when they enter. A printer is spitting out paper. A phone rings. One of the secretaries answers, and another phone rings. Each time, Rollo's stomach lurches a little.

Mrs. Andresson, the one with gold hair and two chins, nods to Mr. Maddox and says, "I'll say you're here." She raps on the door beyond the counter that says S. FERRANTO, PRINCIPAL, opens it, and goes in. When she comes out a moment later, she tells the boys to sit down. "Thank you, Mr. Maddox," she adds.

Mr. Maddox bends over Rollo and looks into his face. Like Coach at the end of the season, he goes to each of them and bends close, but, unlike Coach, he makes no speeches. He only stares, as if he's trying to understand something incomprehensible.

He leaves. The door shuts quietly behind him.

Candy, who's sitting between Rollo and Brig, says, "What do you think?"

"Michon must have told," Rollo says.

"Right." Candy glances at the women working

behind the counter. "What do you think she said?" he asks quietly.

"A bunch of lies," Brig says.

Rollo can't get comfortable on the wooden bench. He crosses and uncrosses his legs. He's hungry again. He watches the women working behind the counter. He wishes Mrs. Andresson would smile at him. He likes her. She never raises a fuss when he needs a pass or forgets his locker key.

They sit there for a long time. People look at them, but nobody talks to them.

– 14 –

Mr. Ferranto blows his nose, then points to the three chairs lined up in front of his desk. They sit down. He puts a cough drop in his mouth, sucks on it for a moment, then slowly reads their names from a piece of paper on his desk. "Julian Briggers. Kevin Candrella. Roland Wingate."

Rollo hates hearing his full first name, especially the way Mr. Ferranto says it, lingering on each syllable. Ro-land. Row land. Probably Mr. Ferranto thinks it's a stupid name, too.

"Mr. Briggers. Mr. Candrella. Mr. Wingate. I have had a very disturbing report about you three." He clasps his hands in front of him on the desk. He has a thick gold ring on one hand, a thick silver ring on the other. "Another student says that this morn-ing, on the third floor, you three assaulted her."

Rollo looks down at the carpet, remembering that when he was a little kid he loved doing somersaults on the carpet in his parents' bedroom. It's a family story that he couldn't say the word and called them "somertallts."

Why is he thinking about that now?

"I'd like to hear what any of you have to say about this," Mr. Ferranto says.

Rollo looks steadily down at the floor. If he doesn't look at Mr. Ferranto, maybe he won't have to answer any questions. But sitting that way makes him feel guilty, and he lifts his head and glances over at Brig.

"Who says we did this?" Brig asks finally.

"I think you know who it is."

"What did she say we did?"

"Mr. Wingate," Mr. Ferranto says. "What do you know about this incident?"

Rollo shakes his head back and forth. His mouth is dry.

"I see. Mr. Candrella, what about you?"

Candy doesn't say anything.

"And you, Mr. Briggers?"

Again, silence.

"I'm warning you, stonewalling me is going to be

counterproductive. I want to know exactly what happened this morning. Who's going to tell me?"

"Nothing happened," Brig says.

In the outer office, Rollo hears voices and the phones ringing. He studies a framed picture on the wall behind the desk. There's Mr. Ferranto sitting on a couch, looking pleasant, with his wife next to him, and their two kids smiling behind them.

Mr. Ferranto coughs heavily. "Maybe I haven't impressed this on you sufficiently, but this is a serious situation. I take it very seriously, and I think you would do well to do the same. Let's start with a simple question: Did you leave the assembly this morning?" He looks at Rollo.

Under Mr. Ferranto's gaze, he can't help nodding.

"You did?"

"I . . . guess so."

"Thank you, Mr. Wingate. All right, you left. And so did you, Mr. Candrella? And you, Mr. Briggers? Why did you all leave?"

"I didn't say I left," Brig said.

"But you did. You were all on the third floor, weren't you?"

"Yes." It's the first thing Candy's said. "We got tired of the play."

"You all got tired of the play at the same moment?"

"You see it every year, the same play," Rollo says.

"So you went up to the third floor, and there you met the other student and assaulted her."

Brig exclaims, "She's a liar! Valerie Michon is a liar and a troublemaker. We did have a slight encounter with her this morning, but it was no big deal."

A slight encounter . . . Rollo almost wants to laugh. Brig says that so precisely and pompously, as if he's the principal. Maybe twenty years from now he *will* be the principal, sitting behind his big shiny desk, his arms folded, giving some kid a hard time. Maybe it'll be Rollo's kid, and Rollo will have to phone his old friend, Principal Briggers. *Brig, give him a break. He's just a kid.* . . .

Brig sits forward on his chair and starts recounting for Mr. Ferranto the things Valerie has done to them over the past few weeks: the harassing phone call, calling them names, and even deliberately stepping on Brig's hand. "She could have broken every bone in my hand," he says.

Mr. Ferranto scribbles on a yellow pad. "This is quite a shopping list of complaints. Am I to infer that, after all this harassment, you decided to teach her a lesson?"

"No." Brig sits back, folding his arms across his chest.

"But you did go to the third floor this morning, and you went after she was there."

"She could have left if she didn't want to be there when we were."

"But she didn't leave, and you were all on the third floor at the same time. And what happened?"

"Nothing," Brig says. "We weren't even there five minutes."

"No, no, no," Mr. Ferranto says, holding a tissue to his nose. "I don't want to hear *'nothing'* again!" He sneezes several times rapidly. "I know something happened." He wipes his streaming eyes. "And you know something happened. Now just tell me what it was. Mr. Candrella!"

"We . . . saw her there," Candy says.

"And? Did you speak to her?"

"No," Brig says. "No, we didn't speak to her."

"You didn't say hello? You didn't ask if she was bored with the play, too? Weren't you interested in talking to her about anything?"

"I'm never interested in talking to her."

"But you approached her. Why did you approach her?"

"No special reason."

"Mr. Candrella, how about you? Do you remember why you approached Miss Michon?"

"Not really," Candy says softly.

"Try to remember, Mr. Candrella. It shouldn't be too hard for a bright young man like you to remember something that happened only a little over an hour ago. . . . What about you, Mr. Wingate? Do you remember?"

Rollo looks up. "Nothing," he says.

"What does that mean?"

His head is hot. "I, uh, don't remember why we, why we approached her."

"Did you speak to her?"

"No." He swallows.

"You just went up to her, grabbed her, and roughed her up, got your hands all over—"

"Is that what she said?" Brig interrupts. "I told you she's a liar."

"Mr. Briggers, I'm telling *you* that I know you three were involved in something unpleasantly close to a sexual assault.

"What!" Brig says. "No way!"

Mr. Ferranto holds up his hand. "Listen to me, all of you. If you know what's best for you, you'll tell me exactly what took place on the third floor this morning. You are not going to get out of this by playing games with me. I expect you to be straight with me. Now . . . Mr. Briggers?"

"Maybe we shook her up a little," Brig says at last.

"Can you be more precise about that?"

"I don't think so."

"Why did you shake her up?"

"She was mouthing off at us. She told us to get the hell out of there, and then she shoved me. And you know, she's no little delicate girl, and that was no little delicate shove."

"So then you took her by the shoulders and shook her?"

"No. I never did that."

"I thought you said you shook her."

"Mr. Ferranto, I said, 'shook her up.' I meant we got her worked up, okay?"

"Well, did you shove her back?"

"We might have."

"Did you pull and tear her clothes?"

"Were her clothes torn?" Rollo blurts in surprise. He doesn't remember that. He doesn't remember the things Brig is saying about Valerie shoving him, either. Is that the way it happened? He doesn't remember exactly how it happened, not the way Mr. Ferranto wants to hear it. *She did this, we did that.* . . .

"If her clothes were torn, she tore them herself," Brig says. "I wouldn't put it past her. That's the kind of person she is."

"You didn't touch her clothes?"

"I wouldn't say that. How do you shove a person without touching their clothes? But she touched mine, too. How come she's not here being cross-examined?"

Mr. Ferranto taps a pencil on the desk. "Miss Michon says you got your hands under her clothing, on her body."

"We didn't do anything like that," Brig says evenly.

"Mr. Candrella, what did you do exactly during this time, while this shoving or pushing and touching of clothes was going on?"

Candy moves around on the chair. "You know . . . I'm not really sure. . . ."

"How about pushing her down to her hands and knees and then trying to—"

Brig looks straight at Mr. Ferranto and shakes his head disbelievingly. "Nothing like that. She's got an imagination!"

"Mr. Briggers. Mr. Wingate. Mr. Candrella." Mr. Ferranto leans forward, speaking slowly and hoarsely. "I hope that you understand how serious this is. Do you understand that you have brought harm to a young woman? That you terrorized her? That you sexually harassed her? That this is a crime? Do you understand that you can be expelled from this school? Do you understand that this can go on your school record and that every college you apply to next year will see that on your record? Do you understand that your whole life might be changed by your mean and thoughtless actions?"

There is silence.

"You know," Brig says at last, "whatever happened, I mean the shoving and stuff, Mr. Ferranto, it was just like a minute or something, that's all."

Mr. Ferranto takes another tissue and wipes his eyes. "I don't see that the time element has much to do with anything, Mr. Briggers." He glances at his watch. "I want you all to go home now. I want you back in school tomorrow, and until that time I don't want you talking about this to *anyone*. Have you got that?"

"Got it," Brig says, already half on his feet.

"Sit down, Mr. Briggers! I didn't dismiss you yet." He looks from one to the other. "Don't misunderstand me, any of you. I'm not through with you people."

TO: DR. SAMUEL WILLIAMS,
    SUPERINTENDENT OF SCHOOLS
FROM: STEPHEN FERRANTO, PRINCIPAL,
    HIGHBRIDGE-UNION HIGH
CONFIDENTIAL

December 21

Dear Sam,

Today, while our student body was in the auditorium for the annual pre-Christmas-vacation assembly, an event took place which I feel I need to inform you about.

During the assembly, four students left without permission. One, a female, who had left first and alone, subsequently complained that she was attacked by the three male students on the third floor of the old building. In addition, she said, they have been harassing her for some time, and this attack was seen by her as a culmination of previous small incidents, one of them clearly sexually tainted.

I have talked to all four students, as well as to one of our secretaries, Patricia Andresson, and to Paul Maddox, head of the English department. The girl initially told her story to Mrs. Andresson, appearing in the front office in some disarray and quite evident distress. Mrs. Andresson urged her to go to the nurse, then to come to me, but the girl insisted that she wanted to talk to Mr. Maddox first. He was called for and spoke to her for a time, which seemed to calm her somewhat. I then spoke to her and received her story. After this, I sent her home. At this time, Mr. Maddox was asked to bring the three boys to my office.

I want to make clear that at the time of the incident, none of these students had permission to be anywhere else. I also want to make clear that my teachers are an outstanding group, but with the best will in the world, it is still not possible to account for every one of our 1,400 students at every moment.

As I see it, we face two problems. (1) To ascertain the truth from the conflicting stories of the three boys and the girl. (2) Damage control.

To be blunt, Sam, the second problem is the one that concerns me most, and frankly, I am torn in two directions.

Background: the girl is one of our gifted and talented students. She does volunteer tutoring work (one on one). She took first place in the county-wide Art Open for the past two years. However, she does have some problems: she's an underachiever (given her IQ scores) and twice this year has been sent to me for inappropriate disagreements with teachers.

The boys are also outstanding: one is on the football team, one president of the student senate, one on the baseball team and president of the honor society. They have never been in trouble before.

After interviewing all of them, the question remains: Was this nothing more than a shoving match brought on by her verbal aggression, or was it an unprovoked sexual attack?

It's clear to me that something did indeed happen. The girl was distraught. Her clothes were in disarray. There is no reason to believe she would fabricate this. The boys admit they were on the third floor. They admit, at the very least, to shoving her around. However, her appearance and general distressed emotional state speak of much more than shoving.

I'm aware of what might be called "the political nature" of this incident. Sexual harassment is very much a topic of the day and I would not like to be accused of taking it lightly. Yet I believe my duties as a principal come first, and I am concerned not to draw unwanted and unpleasant publicity onto our school and our excellent, hardworking faculty. I think it would be *most unfair* if the anxiety of parents was aroused by knowledge of this incident and, as a result, our teachers were accused of lack of concern with student safety. As you know, this very thing happened in another school in our district only two years ago.

I believe that if this situation is not handled carefully, if it's not kept within "the family," so to speak, it could develop into all kinds of unpleasantness. This is the kind of incident the media love to play up for sensational value. In these times of budget cuts and delicate relations with our admittedly hard-pressed parent population, I see publicity about this resulting in *no good* at all.

I want to resolve this incident quickly and quietly, before we close down for vacation day after tomorrow. I do not want to be unfair to anyone in this situation. The fact is, I have no hard evidence. It is the girl's word against the boys. I have mulled long and hard over this situation for the past hours, and here is what I propose: (1) a two-week suspension for the three boys, beginning immediately after winter vacation; (2) that the boys' parents be informed of the incident and asked to take appropriate measures; (3) that the boys be informed in the severest terms that should anything of this nature ever again transpire, the legal authorities will immediately be called in.

I believe this will be fair to all involved and at the same time protect our school and faculty.

Yours sincerely,
Stephen

– 16 –

Candy and Rollo are walking over to Brig's house together. "Brig wants to talk about tomorrow," Candy says.

Rollo nods. They pass a couple of girls waiting for a bus inside a Plexiglas shelter. It's snowing again, a thin gray snow that melts as it hits the sidewalk. One of the girls glances at Rollo, then away quickly, as if she knows him. As if she knows what happened. That's when he remembers the girls he saw when he left Mr. Ferranto's office. Two of them, holding each other and sobbing. Maybe they were crying because they messed up their nail polish. Or forgot their homework. Or failed a test. He doesn't know what they were crying about, he doesn't know them, he doesn't even know their names, but what he thought when he saw them—what he felt convinced of—was that they were crying about Valerie, and that they hated him.

At Brig's house, they get sodas and go out to the garage, where they sit in the car with the motor on and the windows open. Candy's up front with Brig, twirling the dials on the radio. In the back seat, Rollo yawns, his eyes half-closed. If he shuts them, he sees those girls, hugging each other and crying.

"Did Ferranto call your father?" Brig says.

Rollo shakes his head.

"Candy?"

"Mr. Briggers," Candy says, and he's got Mr. Ferranto's voice down exactly, "this is serious indeed. Don't you think I would have conveyed something so important to you?"

Brig laughs and pours soda on Candy's head. Brig's in an excited state, gesturing and talking a lot, talking fast, taking charge. "Ferranto should have told us what Michon said. It's a legal point. We're being accused but not told what we're accused of. Not the details. Right, it's a bunch of lies, but if he hits my father with it—"

"I have a feeling that's in the cards," Candy says.

"Well, damn, don't be so calm about it! You know

what Dr. Briggers will do to me? How can you just sit there and say that?"

"Hey, this isn't calm you're seeing. This is me trying to think about it. What do you think my father's going to do, celebrate?"

"That bitch Michon. Why'd she have to run to Ferranto? Why didn't she just comb her hair and keep her mouth shut? And I'll tell you something else, she had it coming to her. What did we do that was so terrible? We didn't rape her, we aren't a bunch of crazed ax murderers. So we pushed her a little, maybe grabbed some skin. Rollo! Are you grabbed twenty-five times a minute on the football field?"

Rollo nods.

"And what about the locker room? People are always putting their hands on you, right? You're always getting patted on the ass or hit on the side of the head or slapped on the back. Has it ever hurt you?"

Rollo shakes his head.

"Girls act like they're made of glass. What'd she have to get her knickers in such a big twist over? Girls take everything seriously, everything's a major deal to them."

He backs out the car and they drive around for a

while. The streets are dark, the few people out are huddled over, hurrying.

They park in the McDonald's lot and stand outside, scuffing around in the snow. "Do you think we should go to school tomorrow?" Rollo says.

"Yeah, we should go to school tomorrow." In the sickly yellow light of the parking lot, Brig's face looks like wax. "Why wouldn't we?"

"Because . . . you know. Because of what happened."

"Nothing happened. How many times do I have to tell you? Want me to say it again?" Brig leans into Rollo's face. "Nothing. Happened. Candy, back me up, am I right?"

"Sure."

"Tell Rollo."

"He can hear you."

Rollo scratches his name in the snow on the back of Brig's car, *R O L L O,* then wipes it out with his sleeve. "So what are we going to say if somebody asks about it?"

"You? As little as possible. Just keep your mouth shut. We just have to get through this." Brig throws a snowball across the McDonald's parking lot. It smacks into a tree. "Okay, you want to know what to say? We were on the third floor. Michon was on the third floor. There was a little pushing and shoving. That's it."

Rollo leans against the car. He knows he's going to school tomorrow. It's just that he'd much rather stay home and lie around doing nothing, maybe watching some TV, maybe leafing through some old comic books. Whatever.

"You guys talked too much today," Brig says.

"What did I say?" Rollo protests. "I don't think I said anything. Candy, did I say anything?"

Candy smiles, shrugs. His smile is more like a twitch.

Rollo's head feels thick and stiff on his neck. Today was bad in Mr. Ferranto's office, but it would have been worse without Candy and Brig. What if Mr. Ferranto grabs him alone tomorrow? "I have this feeling Ferranto is going to try something," he says. "You know, like divide and conquer. What if he does that? He said he wasn't through with us. What do you think that means?" He grabs Brig's arm.

Brig jerks away. "Rollo, you're getting worked up. You've got to be cool, man."

"Right." His stomach pounds. Is he hungry? When he got home after school that afternoon, he'd been starved. He'd raided the cupboards, shoved chips and sugar cubes in his mouth, a foul combination, but he couldn't stop. Then he devoured two salami sandwiches, washing them down with milk. And he still couldn't stop. He ate noodles, ice cream, cookies. Then he ate supper, because he didn't want to tell his father why he wasn't too hungry.

"So what happened?" he says suddenly. "I mean, what happened up there on the third floor?"

Brig stares at him, as if he can't believe what he's hearing. "Candy, did you hear what this guy just said?"

"Things got a little out of hand," Candy says in his soothing voice. "Just a little out of hand."

"Yeah, right." Rollo lets that information flow into him, says it to himself. *Things got out of hand.* . . . He punches Candy gratefully. Maybe, tomorrow, if he sees those girls who were crying, he'll go over and talk to them. *Look, whatever you heard, I didn't mean anything. Things just got a little out of hand.* . . .

"What are you talking about, Candrella?" Brig says. "Nothing got out of hand, because *nothing happened.* You know, sometimes you talk too much."

Candy laughs with an edge. "I don't think that was me doing all the talking in Mr. Ferranto's office."

"Well, you guys screwed me up. First Rollo, *Yeah, I left assembly.* Then you, *Yeah, we saw her, we saw her in the hall.*"

"I didn't say that."

"You said it. You just about admitted everything. I'm doing a job for all of us, I'm saying, No, nothing happened, and you two are screwing me up. You're saying, Yeah, we were there. And now you, Candy, with your *things getting out of hand* crap. Is that what you're going to tell Ferranto tomorrow? Things got out of hand?" Brig throws several snowballs fast and hard. "Why don't you just tell him we beat Michon up and threw her out the window and have it done with?"

"I like that," Rollo says.

"What, throwing Michon out the window? Me too."

"Candy saying things got out of hand."

"You like that? There's no accounting for taste, is there? I find it stupid." Brig sits down on the back of the car. "I find this whole discussion stupid. Leave it up to you guys and we'd just roll over, go belly up."

Candy's freckles are standing out all over his face. "Bull."

They're barking at each other. All of them are sour and grumbling—scared, Rollo thinks. He is, anyway.

"Ferranto saying we assaulted her," Brig says. "What a bunch of crap! You get assaulted more just walking down the corridor when you're trying to leave school at the end of the day. You can get black and blue walking from homeroom to the front door. We have to get that across to Ferranto. Because if he tells my father these lies, Dr. Briggers'll be down my throat. He'll be down so far, he'll be dancing on my toes."

Rollo bursts out laughing. It's a relief to laugh. Brig grins, finally, and Candy throws an arm over his shoulder. And then they're all laughing, and that fine closeness of friendship is around them, wrapping them up like a big warm blanket, holding them together again. They're going to be all right, Rollo thinks. Everything's going to be all right. Like Brig said, they just have to get through the next day.

– 17 –

Valerie presses herself against a dark wall as they march toward her: a row of huge fish glittering a sinister gold-green and walking malevolently on their tails. Their bodies are separated into three defined sections, and each section on each fish clinks and bends as they come closer. Their smell is unbearable.

She comes awake with a gasp.

She sits up in bed, then falls back against the pillow and looks around her room—tells herself that it *is* her room, that she is here, she is safe. And, resolutely, no matter that it's not light yet and her eyes ache, she tells herself she will get out of bed, take a shower, get dressed, and make coffee for her father.

She will do things. She will not let herself sink.

But she doesn't move.

Little drafts of cool air sweep over her. Her father always sets the thermostat down at night. He says it's wasteful to heat a house full of sleeping and warmly covered human beings. He is concerned about saving energy. He says, If we squander everything now, what will the next generations have?

Up until this very day, she believed—because *he* did—that the world was good, that all she had to do was be herself and never hurt anybody, and everything would be, if not perfect, if not wonderful at all moments, at least very, very good.

If she's not going to get up, she should try to sleep. She should stop thinking. Last night she lay awake for hours, her brain flashing image after image, like a crazed TV. At moments she couldn't breathe. Her throat closed, she sucked in shivery, desperate gulps of air.

And now it happens to her again.

Is this a panic attack?

STOP! The word appears like a red sign in her mind. She wraps her arms tightly around herself, hugs herself into a semblance of composure.

She hasn't yet told her father what happened. Will she? She wants to, but what good would it do? What difference would it make? Isn't she strong enough to hold this inside herself? Why must he be disillusioned and full of sorrow, because something ugly happened to her?

He probably wouldn't even understand. He would say, "Well, why did they do it?" He thinks there is a reason for everything. He believes that the world is a bright and special place. He believes people are good. When she thinks of that now, it is extraordinary. All the years he has lived and not found out how wrong he is! It's amazing. It's enough to make you cry.

She presses her hands against her eyes. *No tears.* She will not allow it. She doesn't dare. If she lets herself go, she's afraid that everything she is keeping so tightly bound inside will burst forth, a torrent that will wash her away and drown her father.

No, she is not going to tell him what happened.

Let him go on sleeping his peaceful, absurd sleep.

– 18 –

"Hey, big Rollo! Big Rollo, big boy." Pete Murando, a kid who's always hanging around, grabs Rollo as he opens his locker. "Rollo! Rollo! Big boy! I heard you're in trouble, big boy, I heard! Take it easy! Don't let them, don't let them—you know, you know!" He punches his fist into his cupped palm.

Pete Murando is a fool. Rollo shrugs him off, but as the morning goes on, it's clear that everyone in school knows what happened yesterday, or at least everyone knows something happened. Guys trail after him. Some of them are winking and grinning, saying his name, hitting him on the back. It's the kind of commotion people make after a game. Like he's a hero.

When he sees Denise Dixon, though, fourth period in Mr. Maddox's class, that's something else. There's a ripple of noise at his entry, and Wendell Smith drawls, "Waaatch out, it's Rooollover Rollo." Some kids snicker, but Denise, sitting in the seat behind his, gives Rollo a long, direct, hard look, the same look she might give a rabid dog in the street. A look that says, *Don't you dare come near me.*

Why that look? He didn't do anything to her. He thinks of saying it. *I wouldn't do anything to you! I wouldn't ever do anything to you.* He sits down and opens his notebook, but what he sees is not his scrawled notes but that cone of white wintry light on the third floor and Valerie standing silhouetted in it. The memory passes through his mind like a dream, with the same vagueness, the same unreality, the same insistence.

"I know vacation is on top of us, but we're going to continue reviewing the novelists and poets we've read this term," Mr. Maddox says, rapping on his desk for attention. He looks at Rollo, frowning as he holds up the literature textbook. "Who remembers what the initials *H.D.* stand for?"

"Hot dog," Wendell Smith whispers. "Right, Rollo baby?"

Mr. Maddox continues talking, but in a few moments he interrupts himself to say, "Mr. Wingate, I want to talk to you. Everyone else turn to page 55 and read the first three paragraphs.

Rollo follows Mr. Maddox out into the hall. "I want you to leave my class." Mr. Maddox says. "I don't think I can teach with you here today."

"Why?" Rollo asks.

"I find it too disturbing to see you sitting here in front of me, and I think you know what I mean. I can't discuss it with you. I think you know that, too. Go down to the office."

Rollo's stomach feels hollow. He doesn't want to be run out of the class. He doesn't want Denise Dixon to see this. He thinks he should smile to show he doesn't care. "What am I supposed to do there?"

Mr. Maddox is scribbling on a piece of paper. "Take this to Mrs. Andresson. She'll give you an answer to bring back to me at the end of the period. Do whatever you want. Just stay there until your next class."

"That's lunch."

"Fine."

"You know, I didn't . . ." Rollo starts.

"What?"

"Nothing." Mr. Maddox has his hands on his hips. His lips are pursed. He isn't going to believe anything Rollo says. "Are you kicking me out forever?" he asks.

Mr. Maddox doesn't answer.

Rollo spends the rest of the period in the office, sitting on the same wooden bench that he sat on yesterday.

"Rollo?" Arica says. "I want to ask you something."

The way she says it, he knows it's about Valerie. He's sitting in a carrel in the library, copying out some stuff for a report for Mr. Maddox that he's supposed to write over vacation.

"Are you busy?" she asks.

"No, that's okay."

Arica leans over the top of the carrel, staring at him. "Rollo."

"Yeah?"

"Is it true?"

"What?"

"What I heard about you and Valerie Michon. Is it true that you raped her?"

"Where'd you hear that? No, it's not true."

"It's all over school. You and Brig and Candy, the three of you."

"No."

"You didn't do that?"

"No."

"You swear to me you didn't? Rollo, tell me the truth."

"I'm telling you, nothing like that."

"You didn't do that?"

"No."

"She's not in school today."

"I don't know anything about that."

"What about Brig? I mean, maybe you didn't, but—"

"No."

She looks at him. "You're telling me the truth?"

"Yes."

"I know you wouldn't lie to me."

"I wouldn't."

"Everybody's saying you raped her."

"No. No way."

"If you say it, I'm going to believe you."

"I'm saying it."

"It's not true?"

"No way, Arica. Nothing like that! Nothing!"

She bites her lip. "Okay, I'm going to believe you."

"You can!"

"Okay." She puts out her hand as if she's going to touch him, then she pulls it back and walks away.

– 19 –

Mr. Ferranto leans across the desk and offers Valerie a mint from a glass jar. "How are you today, Valerie?" he says. "Are you feeling any better?"

She doesn't say yes. She doesn't say no. She doesn't take a mint.

"I know this is hard for you," he says. "For your sake, I want to settle this situation. I want you to put this behind you and go ahead with your life, Valerie. Sometimes bad things happen to people, and it's a shock, but you just have to pick yourself up and get on with it. I know you agree with me."

She doesn't reply.

Mr. Ferranto sighs. "We all need a resolution to

this situation. This is very unpleasant for you, and for me, too. It's good that you're calm," he adds.

Is that what she is, or is it numb? She picks at her thumbnail. This morning she told her father that she had a cold, and she went back to bed, but then Mr. Ferranto had phoned and asked her to come to school. "I need you here," he had said.

"I've given this a great deal of thought," he says now. "I've heard both sides of the story, and I want to be fair to everyone. Have you told me everything, Valerie? Is there anything you want to add or change? Now's the time. Do you want to tell me anything else about what happened and why you think it happened? Do you want to go over it with me again?"

Valerie rips the nail and tears a piece of skin with it. Yesterday she told Mrs. Andresson what they did to her. Then Mr. Maddox. And then Mr. Ferranto, the whole thing again, every sordid little detail. She told him once, and she doesn't want to tell him again. The thought of it makes her sick.

"Well . . . all right, let's go on. My wife, Hela"—he points to the picture behind his desk—"is a psychologist, and I consulted with her about this situation. I started the discussion by a frank relay of the incident.

I hope you don't mind that I spoke to her about it," he adds.

And if she does? Hela Ferranto may be a psychologist, but to Valerie she's just a stranger and, now, one more person who knows what happened to her. She concentrates on her nails, ripping each one carefully with her front teeth, straight across. That's the hard part, to do it straight, not ragged.

"I tried to give my wife a full picture. I explained where I stand. My stand is, I'm concerned about you, but I'm also, of necessity, concerned about the boys. It's my job to look after everyone in this school."

Spurts of heat race through Valerie's head. Phrases of Mr. Ferranto's bounce around in her mind. . . . *my stand is . . . started with a frank relay of . . . concerned about the boys . . .*

"My wife—Hela—pointed something out to me that I'd missed. She pointed out that these boys need to apologize to you."

When Valerie gets through with the nails on her right hand, she starts on the left.

"They need to do it for themselves, and they need to do it for you. You need to hear them apologize. This is what Hela explained to me. They have to be made aware that they've done something terribly wrong, and you need to hear them acknowledging that. Now, Valerie, if I bring them in here to do this, will you accept their apologies?"

She concentrates on her breathing. She read somewhere that if you take in deep breaths, breathe deeply, not shallowly, breathe right down into your belly and let the breath out with a nice regularity, it will slow your heartbeat and give you all sorts of great mental and physical benefits.

"Valerie, sometimes bad things happen, but we can't brood over them. We have to put them in perspective and go on with our lives. Can we agree that we'd like to put this thing behind us and go ahead?"

Should she tell Mr. Ferranto he's repeating himself? She breathes in. She breathes out.

"Valerie, my wife said, and I agree with her, that this is a healing thing to do." He reaches across his desk and presses a button on the intercom. "Mrs. Andresson, I'm ready for them," he says. And before Valerie comprehends what's happening, the door opens and the three boys swagger in.

Valerie leaps out of her chair.

Mr. Ferranto comes swiftly around his desk to stand by her side. She grips the back of the chair. She doesn't look at the boys. It takes every bit of her strength just to stand straight, not to bolt out of the room. Why did Mr. Ferranto do this? Why is he forcing her to be in the same room with them?

"Mr. Briggers," Mr. Ferranto says. "Mr. Wingate. Mr. Candrella. You know that a serious accusation has been made against you three. My investigation leads me to believe that your behavior yesterday, on the third floor, was totally out of line. And whatever happened between you and Miss Michon before that is no excuse!"

Valerie holds tightly to the back of the chair and concentrates on her breathing.

"Now, here is what I am going to do. I am going to inform each of your parents of the situation and they will take whatever action they see fit. Further, the three of you are suspended from school for the first two weeks of the new term."

"Mr. Ferranto, you can't do that!" That's Briggers.

"Be quiet, Mr. Briggers. This is my school, and I won't have such behavior go unpunished. I have one more thing to say to you. If ever there is a similar incident, if ever I hear of any of you being involved in harassing a girl again, I won't hesitate to call in the police." He pauses. "Do you have anything to say? . . . If not, I want each of you to apologize to Miss Michon. Mr. Briggers, you start."

"I can't be sorry if I didn't do anything," he says.

"Mr. Briggers! I won't put up with that arrogance. I'm telling you right now, you're going to do this."

There is another moment's silence, then Briggers says, "Sorry."

"Look at her and say it."

"Sorry!" he raps out.

"All right. You, Mr. Wingate."

"Sorry," comes the mumble.

And before Mr. Ferranto asks him, the third one, Candrella, says quickly, "I sincerely apologize."

"Thank you, Mr. Candrella. That's what I hoped to hear. Valerie, do you accept their apologies?"

They are looking at her, waiting for her to speak, all of them looking at her, all except the fat dumb one, who's looking down at the floor.

"Valerie," Mr. Ferranto says again, "do you accept the apologies of these boys?"

Finally she speaks. "Fuck you all," she says and walks out.

– 20 –

The first day of vacation, Rollo holes up in his room and sleeps. His room is dim, clothes are everywhere. He rolls up in his quilt and sleeps away the hours. He's on his way to sleeping through supper, until Kara appears at his door. "Daddy says come down, Rollo."

"Okay," he mumbles.

"Rollo, wake up! Daddy says it's time to eat. Daddy says put on some clothes and wash your face."

"Okay. . . ."

She pulls the quilt off him. "Daddy says now."

He rolls out of bed and sits numbly for a while. All those hours of sleep have made him groggy. Does he really have to get up? He doesn't want to face his father. He heard him on the phone late last night with Mr. Ferranto. Crap. What now, humble pie? *I'm sorry, I'll never do it again.* . . . But how can you promise a thing like that? How can you be sure what you will or won't do in some future time? Especially when you obviously don't even know what you're going to do right now.

Rollo pulls on his jeans. The whole thing is so unbelievable. Did it really happen? A minute of craziness, stupidity, foolishness—maybe not even a minute, maybe thirty seconds, and everyone is leaping out of their skin, shrieking and screaming, shaking their fingers, stamping their feet, raising their voices. "Adult tantrums," he decides, looking with disgust at his face in the mirror. His eyes are like two little puffy slits.

"Rollo!" His father is calling now, and there's nothing for it but to go downstairs. All through supper he waits for the ax to fall, but it isn't until he's putting his plate in the dishwasher that his father says, "Rollo, come into my study. I want to talk to you."

He doesn't turn around. He doesn't follow his father to the study, either, but instead goes upstairs, closes himself in the bathroom, and brushes his teeth for a long time. After that, he shaves carefully, and all the time he's wondering if it's possible that his father might actually *not* know what happened in school. What if the call last night wasn't from Mr. Ferranto? What if it was from someone else, about something entirely different? And what if his father wants to talk to him because . . . because he's worried about a business problem! *Son, I don't want to alarm you, but times are getting hard, and—*

Dad, don't say another word. I'll go out tomorrow morning and find a job.

Rollo! You're a fine son. A truly good person.

Dad, I'm only doing what anyone would do for his family.

Music rises from downstairs. Kara is probably dancing around the kitchen, waving a dish towel and imagining she's a rock star.

Rollo smooths his finger over his upper lip. His eyes stare back at him from the mirror. Brown eyes, like his father's. Can you see the soul in the eyes, like they say? He looks into those brown eyes and doesn't see anything.

All of a sudden, like a smack in the head, like a hit of electricity, pain travels down the side of his face, rides through his cheekbone into his jaw. Then he seems to hear Coach screaming, *Wingate, you fat, overstuffed fart.* And after that, Mr. Ferranto's voice, *What you did was bad!*

He escapes the bathroom, goes across the hall to his father's room, and dials Brig. "Hello, you've reached the Briggers," Brig's mother says. "At the beep, leave your message for Marcia, Dr. Calvin Briggers, or Julian. If you want the clinic, call—"

He hangs up and tries Candy's number. "Hello!" the senator's deep voice says. "You have reached the residence of Senator Daniel Candrella. No one is home right now. . . ."

Rollo knows that. He knows the Candrellas are in Vail, maybe coming off the slopes this moment. They left early this morning. The Briggerses are gone, too. They took a plane for Orlando, for an unscheduled winter vacation. *They're* probably in the hotel dining room right now, eating a big fancy supper.

After Mr. Ferranto called them, they all decided to clear out of town. The senator was afraid something would leak into the papers. He wanted, Candy said, to be out of the line of fire. As for Brig's father, "He went crazy," Brig said. "He didn't know who he was madder at, me for getting suspended or Ferranto for suspending me."

Rollo finally goes downstairs, but at the closed

door to his father's study he hesitates again. Does he have to go in there? He closes his eyes, wishing he was eleven again, instead of sixteen. And he remembers when he *was* eleven and saw the house and this room for the first time. Then it had been an enclosed side porch, a long narrow room, its windows brushed by the branches of the pines growing outside. He had loved it and wanted it for his own. And suddenly he thinks that if this room had been given to him instead of being turned into his father's study, everything would be different right now. He knows it's an absurd thought, but he can't shake it off.

The door opens. "What are you doing standing out there?" his father says. He points to the ladder-back chair near his desk. "Sit down."

Rollo sits on the floor. He never sits in that particular chair. It used to be his mother's.

His father sits down and stares at him. "Your principal called me, and he told me something I'm having a lot of trouble with. He said there was an incident in school, that you and your friends . . ." His father pauses. "I find this so hard to believe I can hardly say it. . . . Mr. Ferranto said you three . . . attacked a girl."

Attacked . . . He hates that word.

"Is this true?" his father says.

"I guess so," Rollo says, low.

"You guess so? What does that mean, son? Did you do those things to that girl or didn't you?"

Dad, I prefer not to talk about the subject. . . . Rollo looks out the dark window. The pines brush against the glass, like spirits asking to be let in. He shakes his head, then nods.

"Which one, yes or no? You did or you didn't?" his father says.

Rollo wets his lips. "Did." He barely moves his mouth.

"Did," his father repeats. He's tearing a piece of paper into long slivers. "Did," he says again. "You attacked a girl."

"No. We didn't attack her."

"You didn't do it?"

"We didn't *attack* her. It wasn't like that."

"What was it like? It wasn't an attack?"

"No. We just sort of, we sort of shoved, we . . ." Rollo looks down at his hands. Hates his pudgy fingers. "It was no big deal, I don't know what everybody's getting their knickers in such a twist about," he says, repeating Brig's words.

"What?" his father shouts. "What did you just say?"

"Nothing!" His heart is jumping.

"Nothing? No big deal? Three of you and one girl? Where did you learn that? You never saw me doing anything to a woman."

"No," Rollo says.

"I've never laid violent hands on a woman."

"No."

"Why did you do it? Why?"

How can he answer? How can he tell his father what he doesn't know himself? *It's just the way things happen. . . . They happen. . . .* He rolls his head around. He's leaning against the edge of the bookcase and something is jabbing him in the back of the neck. The pain feels good.

His father takes off his glasses, rubs his eyes. "I don't know what to say," he says.

Is his father done? He's just sitting there, rubbing his eyes. Rollo starts to rise, but his father is talking again.

"Do you realize your principal could have called in the police on this? The child welfare people? Do you realize that you could have ended up in the courts, with a record? They could have taken you away."

Rollo shakes his head.

"You didn't know that?"

"No."

"You didn't think about that?"

"No."

"Did you think about the girl? Do you think about anything? Rollo, look at me! This is the way life passes, Rollo. Like *this*." He snaps his fingers. "It seems long to you now, but it's not. It goes fast. And you only get one chance at it, that's why you've got to *think*. You've got to *think* about what you're doing, and you've got to live right."

Rollo nods. He's remembering running up the stairs after her . . . seeing the black silhouette of her in front of the window . . . like a cutout . . . and then what they did, all that crazy thrilling stuff. . . .

"Right now you think life is forever. You think time is endless. You don't have a sense of urgency. You think you can do anything and it doesn't matter. That's not true. *Everything matters*. It matters to you. It matters to the other person. Do you understand what I'm saying?"

Rollo nods again.

"Do you have anything to say? Anything at all?"

Sure he does. If his father wasn't yelling at him and going crazy with lecturing, Rollo could tell him things . . . about being with his friends and how good it feels and how you never want that good feeling to stop and how that's why you do things sometimes that maybe aren't so smart.

But his father wouldn't understand, anyway.

His father doesn't know about things like crapping around and making jokes and all the dumb stuff he and Candy and Brig do that's just . . . *good*. Just part of being friends.

"What you did was thoughtless, stupid, vicious. The least you could be is sorry."

"Okay." Why does his father have to call him names?

"Okay? Is that all you can say? Don't you feel anything for that girl, for what you did to her? Rollo! What kind of person are you? I don't see anything on your face, no feeling, nothing."

Rollo stares at the floor and thinks about his friends, about always knowing you have somebody in your corner, and how your friends never let you down, and how they never make you feel like shit. Like he feels now.

"I never thought I'd say this, but I'm glad your mother's not here now." His father's voice thickens. "I'm glad she's not here to know that her son would do such a thing."

Rollo scrambles to his feet, his face burning. He hates his father for saying that.

"I'm not finished," his father says as Rollo reaches

for the doorknob. "I'm not finished with you or this subject!"

Rollo waits, standing by the door, but he doesn't hear anything else his father says, and he doesn't look at him. There's only one thing he wants now. He doesn't want to break down and cry in front of his father.

– 21 –

*Dear Great Listener . . . dear Someone . . . whoever you
are . . . are you there? Are you listening? Great Spirit!
Big Ear! Listener! Whatever you are, please . . . give me
a sign. Do you hear me? Can you hear me? Will you
hear me?*

Valerie pauses and draws in a breath. She's in the
room behind the kitchen, which her father calls his
office. Maybe it was a pantry once. No windows. Just
a tiny room with a desk and floor-to-ceiling shelves
overflowing with books and paper. She's sitting in
front of the computer, writing something, maybe a
letter. They're words, anyway, a spill of words like
water pouring over a dam.

Dear Big Ear, did it ever occur to you that there are

things missing in this world? Things absent. Things not in place. Things gone. Things like justice and sanity and kindness and care. People should be kind to each other, but instead they're cruel and hurtful. Okay, I know, I'm indicting the whole world because of three boys. Sorry, but it's the way I feel.

I want to know why it happened. I was standing at the window, looking out at the woods. I was going to go in the art room and work, and then they were there, and they did things to me nobody has a right to do to another person, and nothing has been done to them in return. Two-week suspension? Baby stuff. I don't call that anything.

SOMETHING WICKED THIS WAY COMES.

She stares at the screen. All on their own, her fingers have typed those words. SOMETHING WICKED THIS WAY COMES. Where did that come from? Something Mr. Maddox once read them? She types again. *SOMETHING EVIL THIS WAY CAME.*

She breathes, calming herself, remembering the day she ran on to Mr. Maddox about the Great Universal Spirit. Is there really Something out there, a transcendent, overarching spirit? She has always believed it. She has to go on believing it. Otherwise, everything is too meaningless, too absurd.

In the kitchen, she hears her father moving around. In a few minutes he will call her to supper. Later he'll come in here and use the computer himself. They've always shared it, always respected each other's privacy. He would never look at anything in her files without her permission. But what does it matter if she's private or not? He knows what happened. Sort of. Mr. Ferranto called and told him.

She didn't want that to happen, but it did, and then he came to her, her dear unworldly father, and he said, "Val . . . sweetheart . . . your principal called." His face was pale. He took her hands. "What happened? What did they do to you?"

How to tell him? She'd always protected him, looked after him as much as he looked after her. Was it a bargain they made a long time ago or something she had decided on?

She paced . . . and she told him, but she didn't tell him the way it really had been. She used words like *grab* and *push,* as if that were all of it. She said, "Yes, three boys . . ." and shrugged, as if they were no more than three cutups, three clowns who got a little wild and out of control. She made less of what happened, much less.

He wanted to know about the boys, and what did Mr. Ferranto say? Were they being punished? When she told him, "Suspended for two weeks," he nodded approvingly. Then he looked at her again, and held her hands, and said, "Are you really all right?"

She nodded. Oh, yes, yes. But there was something about the way he asked her that, and the way he looked so sorrowfully and carefully into her face, that almost brought her to tears. She wouldn't cry, though. She wouldn't let herself. Not in front of him. "I'm fine," she said. "I was shaken up, but now I'm fine, I'm really fine."

She wants to believe that.

She starts typing again.

I know they say it's good to talk . . . shouldn't keep things locked up inside yourself . . . but who do I talk to? Not my father.

Janice? She's too flakey.

I've thought about Mark, but that's crazy. I don't know him that well. What makes me think he'd even understand? And what if he said, Did you yell, Valerie? Did you order them to stop? Did you defend yourself? Did you hit them? What were you doing up there, anyway? I don't want to hear those questions!

Big Ear, better listen while you have the chance, because I can wipe these words out in one split second. Too bad I can't put my feelings up on the screen and wipe them out just as fast. I hate the way I feel. I keep wanting to cry, don't want to get out of bed in the morning, think about being an artist and know it'll never happen. . . .

When am I going to feel good again?

When am I going to stop thinking about it?

Big Ear, are you listening? There's something else I need to get off my chest. Before this happened, I never wanted to even think about things like this. I wouldn't read the stories in the paper or watch them on TV. I said to myself, Nothing to do with you, Valerie. . . . I thought it was a different class of person things like this happened to. Someone who wasn't so smart or did something wrong or lived in a bad place. . . .

What I think now is that you don't have to be dumb or live anyplace special or do anything wrong to have it happen to you. You can be minding your own business, just looking out a window, and it happens. Just standing there, and it happens.

It happens. And nobody knows what it feels like until it happens to them.

− 22 −

Rollo is watching TV; at least, he's staring at the screen. He's hardly moved for the past hour, except to push the button on the remote. He keeps looking at the clock, waiting for Kara to come in from work. For two days now, she's the only person who's acknowledged his existence.

His father acts as if Rollo has ceased to be someone real. He doesn't seem to see Rollo. He definitely doesn't talk to him. He walks around him as if he's not there. He doesn't even notice him when Rollo sits across from him at the table. It's not that his father's distracted or busy or thinking about other things. He doesn't have any difficulty with Kara. He notices her reading a new Nancy Drew, he asks her what chapter she's on, discusses the plot enthusiastically with her, and then goes off with her for a walk. Only Rollo gets the silent *you are not my son you might as well be dead* treatment.

Rollo's thoughts, addressed to his father, go like this. *You don't understand, Dad, but I'll try to tell you how it can happen that you do something not so great . . . okay, something rotten. Right, I agree. Let's call it rotten and vicious. The thing is, you're not thinking, even if on one level you know what you're doing isn't right. The thing is, there's something in you that's saying, Don't think about it . . . so you don't, and that's easy, because you don't want to think about it, anyway, you don't want to say something and be a jerk, you just want to do what your friends are doing. So you do it. You do what they're doing, you grab the girl and . . . you do all those things. . . . Okay, maybe later your stomach sort of turns and you feel sort of amazed and ashamed and sort of sick of yourself, but you're not, suddenly, somebody a person can't see or talk to, you're not suddenly a monster. . . .*

The phone rings then, and as Rollo is trying to decide if he'll answer it or not, Kara walks in the door. "I'll get it," she yells. "Nobody else! Hello!" he hears her say. "This is Kara! Who is this?"

It's probably a sales pitch for aluminum siding.

"Hang up, Kara," he calls. "You know what to tell them."

He hears her say, "No, we don't buy anything over the phone. Good-bye!" She comes in, sits down next to him, and gives him a kiss on the neck.

She looks cute as hell. She's wearing black tights, a skirt printed with gold butterflies, a black T-shirt, and a big yellow bow in her hair. "How was work today?" he asks.

"Good and bad. A man hit his little boy. I said, 'Don't hit him!' Then he was mad, he said, 'Mind your own business,' then Carl said, 'What is the problem? Is everything all right? Go back to work, Kara.' " She hugs Rollo's arm. "You wouldn't hit a boy or a little teeny fly, even."

"Kara, I kill flies all the time."

Kara ignores the interruption. "I was sad because the man was mean to his little boy. I tried to make my head forget, but it wouldn't. See!" She wipes her eyes. "I'm sad right now, and then I have to cry and my life is ruined."

He wishes she would stop talking. He wishes he was someplace else. He wishes the thing in school had never happened and that Valerie Michon lived a thousand miles away and that he had never even heard her name.

"Rollo?" Kara takes him by the chin and holds his face tenderly. "Rollo, are you sad, too?"

For a moment, for a fraction of a second, he wants to tell her . . . *everything*. He wants to let the words roll out, he wants to say it all. Let Kara hear, because no matter what he says to her, no matter what he tells her, to her he will still be her perfect brother.

Her face is right near his. She is looking at him with her truthful eyes. His lips go dry. He's wrong. Wrong again. How could he think, even for an instant, of telling Kara? To tell her would be just one more disastrous thing. She is retarded, but she isn't stupid.

— 23 —

"I swing," Keefer yells from the couch, "Valerie, I swing, too. Me. My turn."

Valerie gives Keefer's older brother one last twirl, then picks up the little girl by the hands and swings her out and around in a wide circle. Keefer screams wildly.

"They're a couple of hellions," their mother said when she asked Valerie to baby-sit them over winter vacation. "Do you think you can stand them for whole days at a time?"

Mrs. Brunet manages a kids' clothing store. She pays Valerie really well. The money is great, but the money isn't what counts now. Valerie would take care of Wick and Keefer for free—she'd pay Mrs.

Brunet for the privilege—because when she's with the kids they keep her so busy it's almost impossible to think about anything else.

She doesn't want to think about a lot of things.

Like Mark Saddler and that awkward phone call last night. "Hey, Val," he said, "how's the girl?" He's never called her at home before. They carried on for a strained few minutes before she hung up. Does he know? It's possible. *Possible?* Sure he knows. Everyone in school knew in two seconds flat. Maybe, in his way, Mark was being considerate, letting her know he was on her side. Or maybe he just wanted some titillating details.

The numb sweatiness starts again. Her hands prickle—the back of her hands and the tips of her fingers. Don't think about it. . . . Forget it. . . . Then the questions begin. Why weren't there any words? She can't remember any words. What's the meaning of that? What's the meaning of anything that happened? Why did they do it? Why did they do it to her?

She keeps thinking, if only she understood she would be able to stop having crazy emotions. Last night, after Mark called, she had gone into the backyard and smashed plates against a tree, then picked up the broken pieces and smashed them again until there was nothing left.

The kids are running in circles, screaming and giggling, running around a chair, chasing each other. Keefer, who, at three, adores her brother, screams his name, "Wick Wick Wick Wick," in a shrill, unrelenting cacophony of love, her plump hands out to catch him. He runs from her, giggling, impish. "Can't catch me! Can't catch me!"

"Wick Wick Wick!"

"Can't catch me! Can't catch me!"

He flings himself at Valerie. "Save me from the Keefer monster!"

Valerie touches his sheaf of dark silky hair. His warm little paw is on her leg. Will he still be so sweet when he grows up? Is it possible those other three had been little boys once, sweet-smelling little boys with big brown eyes?

She tells them they're going outside and they all start picking up toys and throwing them into the yellow plastic toy baskets. "We don't want your mom to go crazy when she comes home and sees the living room a big mess," Valerie encourages them.

"Yeah! Mom go crazy," Keefer agrees happily.

They crawl around the floor, picking up toys. Suddenly, Wick jumps on Valerie's back.

"I'm a cowboy and you're my horse." He kicks her in the sides with his sharp little heels. And now all the effort Valerie has put into *not thinking about it* is for nothing. It's happening again, like a fast forward on the VCR, the images blurring, but everything there.

Her mind spares her nothing. The three of them marching toward her . . . crowding her . . . the sudden rush of hands, the hands, hands everywhere . . . and then she's down and one of them is trying to get on her.

"Get off me!" she screams. She shakes Wick off and stands up, stands over him. "Don't you dare do that!"

There is silence. The little boy stares at her. The little girl sucks on her fingers.

Valerie is trembling. Abruptly she remembers something that happened yesterday. She was walking past the corner of Seneca and Saratoga streets when a man sitting in the bus shelter greeted her. "Happy New Year, darlin'!" He wore a black cap, had a scarf wrapped around his neck. Maybe he was drinking. Maybe he was just being friendly.

What she remembers is her shock, her fear. How she hurried on, her shoulders pinched, her stomach throbbing. What she thinks is that *before* she would have shrugged or smiled. She would have felt safe. She would have said, "Happy New Year to you, too, you're a few days early."

The attack has changed her. They did it and they left, and they left something behind, and not just her picking herself up from the floor. They left her changed. Before, she always felt brave and alert and interesting—all kinds of positive things. Oh, sure, the negatives were there sometimes, the bad feelings, but they came and went. They didn't stay. Now something stays with her, something gray and ugly that was never there before. It's like something hard and stony. It's lodged itself inside her. It's got claws and teeth and it chews on her. It makes her feel scared and mean.

She looks at Wick and holds out her arms. The little boy slowly comes to her. He lets her hold him.

"Valerie, me too," Keefer says. "Me, a hug, too."

"You too," Valerie says and draws both children close.

– 24 –

Walking home after delivering some stuff of his father's to the cleaners, Rollo turns onto Mount Pleasant Avenue, a hilly street of large old Greek revival houses. Snow is mounded along the roads and melting off the roofs in the sun. A cold clear day. Good skiing weather, but Rollo doesn't have anyone to ski with. He hasn't done a thing this vacation but sit around and stare at the TV. All in all, it hasn't been the greatest vacation, and it doesn't help that his father is still mad at him, still not talking to him.

"I'm not finished with you," his father had said ominously, the night he called Rollo into his study. Since then Rollo has gotten the silent treatment. Is that his punishment, or is there something else his father is going to do? How long does he need to make up his mind? That blank face his father shows him is worse than any punishment. If he has something else in store for Rollo, why doesn't he do it and get it over with! Then Rollo can start living like a normal human being in a normal family again.

That's what he's fuming about as he turns onto Mount Pleasant Avenue and notices a girl coming down the hill toward him. It takes him a moment to realize it's Valerie.

He stops.

It's unmistakably her—a tall, gawky figure in a long coat. She's got two little kids with her, and she's lifting one of them over a snowbank.

Seeing her is a shock to Rollo. She's big, solid, her face is full of color. Sunlight glints off her glasses. And yet there's something unreal about her. No, what's unreal is seeing her here, outside, in the world, moving, striding down the hill. He hasn't thought about her since school, hasn't let himself think about her. And now here she is, coming straight toward him. Maybe that's why he stumbles, loses his footing, and falls. He goes down on the sidewalk like a kid.

He hops up, brushes himself off.

She sees him.

She stops dead and stares. Then she turns

abruptly, pushes the kids up the steps of a white house, herds them inside, and slams the door.

This is the beginning of something Rollo can't explain.

When he gets home he looks up Valerie's address—only one Michon in Highbridge—and discovers it's Academy Street, not Mount Pleasant Avenue. Maybe she's baby-sitting the two kids. Maybe they're relatives. He locates Academy Street on the town map his father has tacked up in the garage, and the next morning he goes out to find it.

Her house is on one of the older streets near the canal. A street of little houses with peaked roofs and tiny windows. He doesn't stop or anything. He just looks at the house and goes by. Then he walks over to Mount Pleasant Avenue, and he doesn't stop there, either. Just walks up the hill.

But later he calls Valerie's number, then hangs up at the first ring. He does that a few times. Dials and hangs up on the first ring, before anyone answers. The next day he walks past her house again. In fact, he walks past her house and the house on Mount Pleasant Avenue two or three times that day.

What is he doing?

He's not sure, but he thinks if he sees her, he'll talk

to her. Maybe *she'll* want to talk. He'll listen. He's a good listener, probably a better listener than talker. He's definitely not a great talker, though he can usually find something to say. Anyway, they'll have a conversation. It doesn't have to be long. Maybe that's the first thing he'll tell her. *We can just talk for a few minutes.* They'll talk about ordinary stuff like the weather or Mr. Maddox or football, whatever she wants to talk about.

The next time he dials her number, he doesn't hang up, and she answers. "Hello . . . ?" He puts the phone down quietly. *Hello . . . ?* He goes on hearing her voice long after he's hung up.

Then he knows why he called her. He wanted to hear her voice. He wanted to hear her say something normal and nice.

Later he goes out again, walks the mile or so to Academy Street. It's dark, and when he comes to her house, instead of passing by, he slips along the side of the garage, through deep snow, past a tangle of frosted bushes and around into the backyard. He stands in the darkness and looks into a lighted window. He sees a table, a stove, a calendar on the wall. A bald man appears in the square of yellow light. He's fat and dressed in a mechanic's gray jumpsuit.

Valerie enters the room. Rollo moves closer to the

house, and as he does, something lands on his head. His heart kicks against his ribs, but it's only a lump of snow that slid off the roof. In the house, the man hands Valerie a plate of food. She sits down and begins to eat. Suddenly she looks out the window, seems to look straight at him. Again his heart kicks hard, and he leaps aside into the darkness. Did she see him? What if she comes rushing out of the house at him—what will he say? What excuse will he have? He can't explain why he's there. He doesn't know himself.

The next time he sees her, it's around six o'clock and he's on his way to meet Kara at work. As he opens the door to the restaurant, Valerie and the same two kids come out. He almost bumps into her.

She stares. Her face floods with color, and she pushes past him.

He goes after her. "Valerie," he calls.

She turns, swinging around so violently her glasses fall off. The little kids are gaping at him. She kneels and fumbles around in the snow. He hurries forward and picks up her glasses. "Here," he says. "I've got them."

"Why are you following me?" she says.

"No . . . I'm not."

"I know you are!" She raises her arm, and for a moment he thinks she's going to hit him.

She snatches the glasses from him, takes the kids by the hands, and rushes away. She's almost running, lifting the kids off the sidewalk. They're wearing red jackets and look like two low-flying balloons.

– 25 –

"Hello, Valerie?" she hears.
"Yes?"
"This is Rollo Wingate."
She hangs up.

"Hello, Valerie, I don't want to bother you, I just want to talk to you for a—"
She hangs up.

"Hello, please don't hang up."
"We have nothing to talk about." And she hangs up.

* * *

He calls again. He says, "I don't want you to hate me." She looks at the phone in her hand and considers this amazing statement. It would be no less amazing if he'd said, *I want you to be my best friend.* She hangs up.

The next time he calls, he says, "Hello, guess what—"

"What do you want?"

"—this is Rollo Wingate again," he finishes lamely.

"What do you want?"

"I just want to talk to you. I don't want you to hate me," he says again.

"I don't hate anybody."

"Thank you!"

Her eye throbs. His jubilation is unbearable. "You're the one who hates," she says quietly.

"No, no, I'm like you, I don't hate any—"

Her reserve breaks. "How dare you say that? You are not like me! I've never hurt another person in my life. Not the way you and your friends—" She stops herself and hangs up.

Valerie skates slowly alongside Wick and Keefer. It's a bright, sunny day, and the pond is packed with people. She takes Keefer by the hands and starts pulling her around on the ice. "Come on, slowpoke!" She skates backward, pulling the little girl across the pond. Then Wick has to have his turn. Finally she says, "Okay, guys, skate on your own for a while now."

She stands by the gate, watching them, ready to race out if either one needs rescuing.

"Hello," someone says behind her.

She turns pleasantly, not immediately recognizing the voice, but when she sees who it is, her chest becomes a knot of frozen breath. "Wick! Keefer!" she yells, moving out on the ice. "Come on! Off! We're going home!"

She sits them down on a bench to put on their boots.

He's leaning against the gate. Is he watching her? He's got ice skates on, but he's not going out on the ice.

"Keefer, let me help you." Valerie bends over the child, who's tugging at her sock. "We have to hurry."

"No," Keefer says. "Me I self do it."

"Hi, again." The bench creaks as he sits down on the other end.

Although the whole width of the bench is between them, he's too near. A chill presses against her back, as if she's feverish. If he tries to touch her, she'll kill him.

"Listen, what we were talking about the last time—" He just starts talking, as if she were waiting for him.

"We weren't talking about anything," she says, not looking at him. "Go away. Stop bothering me."

"Who's that guy?" Wick asks.

"I just want to say one thing," he pleads. "Okay?" She doesn't answer.

"I never would have done—I mean, if I'd known you, I never would have—"

"If you'd known me," she repeats. "You're saying that a girl you know is safe. But a girl you don't know . . . you and your friends can come along and do anything you want to her."

"No! I didn't mean that! I was only trying to explain that it was different then. I mean, now I've talked to you, and I can see you're different than I thought, and if I'd known you then—"

She can't stand this. She can't stand what he's saying, his stumbling excuses, his blindness. His dumbness. His density. If he'd known her—what a horrible, terrible, crass, frightening thing to say.

"Valerie . . ." He's almost whispering. "I'm not a bad person. Honest. People tell me I'm a nice guy."

He's stupid, she decides, pulling Keefer's boot on. Wick has ambled away to watch the skaters.

"I didn't know it would be like that. It was just—it was my friends, and—I didn't have anything against you."

She wants this dopey, moronic guy to shut up, *now*.

"Remember when I said I was sorry? I meant it. Are you listening? Could you say something to me?"

"Okay, I'll say something. There was this guy, not too smart, who hit another guy over the head with a baseball bat," she says rapidly. "Why? Because he felt like it. He woke up one morning and he wanted to hit somebody over the head, so he did."

"I wouldn't," he says quickly.

"After he hits the other guy over the head, he goes back to him and says, 'Gee, fella, won't you talk to me?' He can't understand why the guy who's got the lump on his head doesn't want to talk to him, or see him, *or even know he exists*."

"No," he says, "it wasn't like that. It wasn't. I mean—no weapons."

"No," she says. "Just hands."

- 26 -

Now that he's talked to Valerie, there's only one thing he feels certain of in all the tangle of his thoughts, one idea he keeps coming back to: if only it hadn't happened.

If only he hadn't followed Brig.

If only he had stopped on the stairs.

If only he had said something. *What're we doing. . . . Why are we doing this. . . . Hey, guys. . . .*

If only he had looked at his hands and known that what those hands did was what he did, that they were attached to him, they were *him*.

If only life was like a movie you put on the VCR, and you could roll back time, make what happened unhappen. Flip REVERSE and watch all the parts you didn't like jumping back in a blur.

The three of them walking backward down the corridor . . . prancing backward down the stairs . . . falling into their seats in the auditorium . . .

Then he'd take the tape and snip off that bit, so they could never go forward the old way again. Instead, they would sit in the auditorium and watch the play straight through. They would be there as the curtain fell, they would applaud the actors, and when the lights went on, they would stand up and stretch and complain about how many times they had already seen this play.

They would be unaware of Valerie on the third floor, looking out the window.

And none of them would ever notice the difference in the tape. All that would be missing would be those few minutes.

– 27 –

Valerie's in her bedroom, writing in her journal. "Something has been taken from me. Something has been *stolen*. My sense of safety in the world, my bravery. They belonged to me. And somebody's stolen them. Three thieves—"

The phone rings. She stiffens. She doesn't know how she knows, but she knows it's *him*, one of the thieves. She stares at the white phone on her desk. She'd let the phone ring forever, but her father takes it downstairs, and in a moment he calls up, "Val, for you."

She picks up the phone.

Over the wire comes his nasal, uneasy breathing. "I was thinking about what you said at the pond.

About the guy who hits the other guy? I thought, uh, we could talk about it."

She glances up, catches herself in the mirror, eyes narrowed, shoulders hunched venomously into the phone. Consciously, she leans back and assumes a softer posture. She doesn't want to become that person she sees in the mirror. It would only be one more thing they have done to her.

"You don't want to talk about it?" he says into her silence. "That's cool. We can talk about other stuff. My father says life is short, and even if I don't feel it now, I have to remember that. He said I have to have a sense of urgency."

For a moment she wouldn't mind talking about that. The idea of urgency is interesting. Is it really true that life is short? To her, it seems as if life is endless and time is forever. A week reaches to the horizon, a month stretches so far she can't even see the end of it. Take this vacation—it's been going on so long! And she's still feeling so bad. When will all this end? Will it ever end? What's short about this?

She drops the phone. She doesn't want to talk about life or time or *anything* with Rollo Wingate. Why did she let him babble on? He's done it again, tramped into her life without being asked. All she wants is to forget what happened, forget him and everything about him and his friends, and he's making it impossible.

"Valerie . . . ?" She hears his voice from the dangling phone and bangs the receiver into the cradle.

Her father comes up the stairs. "Who was that on the phone? Look." He fondly holds up his latest invention, a combination alarm clock–thermometer. The idea is that when you wake up, you know instantly what the weather is. "I think I've got some of the bugs worked out. This could change a person's whole outlook on life."

She nods and he passes by. Then she can't sit still. That abstracted look of her father's . . . his not-real interest in who called . . . he didn't even wait to hear her answer. She circles the room restlessly. All at once she wants to run after him, sees herself doing it— running, yelling. *Wipe that smile off your face!*

She looks out onto the dark street, trying to compose herself, not succeeding. Does he ever hear anything she says? Does he see anything but his workshop? How has he lived with her these past days and not even noticed how unhappy she is? He knows what happened to her! What does he think, one little discussion, and everything is peachy-keen?

"Dad!" she shouts suddenly. "Dad!"

"What is it?" He comes to her door, looking alarmed.

She's all set to blast him, all set to wipe that anxious smile off his face, to tell him some hard home truths. And then she stops. She can't do it. It's unfair; she was the one who protected him. Her choice. What had she said to him after Mr. Ferranto called? *It was nothing, Dad, really, just a prank, some shoving. . . . Three jerky boys . . . No, I'm fine. . . .*

"What is it?" he says again.

She raises her shoulders. "One of those boys keeps calling, trying to talk to me. What should I do? I think he wants me to forgive him."

"And do you want to?" he says.

It's such a nice sensible question—and she seems to know the answer. No, she doesn't want to forgive him! Why should she forgive, why should she forget? Why make it easier for him? Why take away his pain—will that take away hers?

In the morning, waking is like climbing out of a pit. A nightmare of the clanking fish pursues her out of sleep.

She stares at the ceiling. *Do you want to forgive him? No! No! No!* But the answer doesn't satisfy her this morning. The *No* isn't good enough. It doesn't release her. She wants what happened in school—the attack, the assault—to be done with, and it isn't. It doesn't go away. It doesn't end.

She gets up, takes a shower, gets dressed. She tells herself she's not thinking about it, she's not thinking about Rollo Wingate, the thief. But all the time a voice in her mind is whispering, *To err is human, to forgive divine*. "I won't!" Valerie cries. Forgiveness is fine for angels, but she's not in the angel league. It isn't that her wings are clipped—she doesn't *have* any wings. If she did, she would fly herself out of this pain. She would end it. Isn't there something she can do? "Please," she whispers.

He calls again that morning. She's eating breakfast. No place to go, as Mrs. Brunet has closed the shop until after the New Year and is home with the kids herself.

"Hello, Valerie, this is Rollo. Before you hang up," he says hastily, "I just want to ask you one thing."

She takes a bite of toast, spits it out, bangs down the phone.

He calls again immediately. "I was hit by lightning once. It was a long time ago at a lake where my parents rented a cottage. I was three years old, sitting in my mother's lap, watching a storm coming in, and then, zap!"

This is so bizarre, she waits.

"My mother took the main hit, because she was in contact with the metal chair. She was knocked right off the chair, me with her. Remember I said I had a question?" He starts talking fast. "Well, I'm going to ask, even if you say no. Would you meet me and talk to me? I just want to say something to you. I know you're going to say no, but could you just think about it? Okay?"

She doesn't say no. She doesn't say yes. She doesn't respond in any way—she can't—she couldn't even if she wanted to. Something is happening to her. Although she's still sitting in the same place at the kitchen table, with the phone in her hand, all that's around her has become vague, and all that she sees is an image in her mind. A mother and a child in a chair. Then the child in the chair alone. The image takes her over . . . takes her away . . . seizes her.

She's nearly trembling. The phone drops from her hand. A nervous quivering grips her, a joyful nervous twanging of her senses, the complete and true opposite of the grayness that has oppressed her for so many days now. She leans back, raising her arms.

She will make a sculpture. She sees it complete . . . and completed. It will be in two sections, two separate scenes joined by a single base: a mother and a child on one side in a rocking chair; on the other side, the chair again . . . the child alone.

She starts sketching on a napkin. The base will be more than its physical self, more than clay, it will stand for the meaning of the whole sculpture: how everything is linked, how nothing stands alone, how "before" and "after" are all part of a single entity, a single experience, an ongoing thing that is Life.

Her chair comes down with a bang. Oh, God, is she being pretentious? Maybe, but she doesn't really care. Her fingers are tingling. Already she can feel the damp, heavy texture of the clay. Already she's mulling over problems of proportion. Already she knows this will be different from anything she's ever done, more complicated and yet more focused, more challenging, more satisfying, more *everything*.

Then, in another startling moment, staring at the napkin, she understands that the sculpture will be a metaphor for what happened to her. Before that morning on the third floor, she had been like a child safe in its mother's arms, in the arms of the world, which promised her only good things. Then lightning struck: sudden, unexpected, destructive—and she was left alone, bereft.

He's still talking. She can hear his voice coming out of the receiver. She picks it up. "I don't think my mother suffered any aftereffects from the lightning," he's saying. "She died when I was ten, but that was something else. Car accident, the other driver was drunk. . . . I miss my mother. I love her. She was, you know, special."

For a moment she lets in sympathy for him, like light under a drawn shade. She misses her mother, too, but differently: she doesn't remember her mother—how could she? What she probably misses is *a* mother. She works on the idea of the chair. The pencil sinks into the soft paper, and she looks for something else to sketch on.

"What about your mother?" he asks.

She starts drawing on a brown bag. "What about her? She's dead." She makes another sketch of the chair, very simple, almost a single line. She should end this conversation, but she doesn't, because something quick and glad is flowing through her. She is full of light: everything is light inside her. Even Rollo can exist in this light.

"Did she die in an accident, too?" he asks.

"Childbirth."

"I didn't think things like that still happened. Was she very young?"

"Twenty."

"Neither of us have mothers," he says, as though

it's an amazing coincidence. But the only amazing thing here is that the raw material for what she already knows is going to be the best sculpture she's ever done was given to her by him. And for that, she can't help feeling grateful. Maybe that's why, when he asks her again to meet him, she hears herself saying yes.

Rollo looks across the table at Valerie. "You want anything else?" She's barely touched the cup of hot chocolate she ordered.

"What am I doing here?" she says.

He doesn't really know. He didn't think this through too well. His only thought had been that if they could meet, if she would sit and talk to him in a sort of normal and ordinary way, it would make a difference. He's not a monster—that's all he wants her to see.

"You could have a piece of pie," he says, and digs into the hot peach pie in front of him. A gob of vanilla ice cream slides across the top. He forks pie into his mouth, then a lump of ice cream. It's good, and he doesn't stop until his plate is just a smear of sticky crumbs.

Valerie is staring at him. She's sitting on the edge of the seat, one leg out in the aisle, her coat around her shoulders, as if she's ready for a speedy takeoff. "I thought you wanted to tell me something. What's the point of this meeting?"

"No point." He laughs nervously. "I just wanted you to see that I'm a nice guy."

Her cheek twitches. "Right. A nice guy who gets his kicks out of attacking girls."

"I don't," he says morosely. He already said he was sorry, but maybe he should say it again. He *is* sorry. He's gotten more and more sorry with each day. He could just say, in a dignified way, *I apologize, Valerie. I truly and sincerely* . . . What if she did something solemn, like putting her hand on his head? *Go in peace, Rollo Wingate. I forgive you.* Maybe he should say that. *I hope you forgive me. . . . I deeply regret and sincerely hope* . . . "You want to hear how it happened, you want to hear my story?" he blurts.

"Your *story*?" She pushes aside her cup, and cocoa sloshes into the saucer. "You think what you did is a *story,* your version or mine? You tell me yours and I'll tell you mine? Maybe you think I'll like your story better than mine. This is not equal time," she goes on, her voice thickening. "Something happened to me. You know what it was, and I know what it was. There is no *story*."

Her nose is red at the corners. Is she going to cry? He shoves his napkin across the table to her. This is not working out right. His idea was so simple, just two people sitting around talking, maybe even having a good time.

She's biting her lip, swallowing. She doesn't touch the napkin. "You trapped me, you held me, you didn't let me move," she says. "You got your dirty hands all over me—" Her voice breaks. "No, I'm not crying," she says, wiping her face with her sleeve. "Don't you worry, I'm not crying."

Why did he start this? Why did he ask her to meet him? What was on his mind? He can't remember now. He's sweating, and the pie in his stomach is like a block of cement.

She sits straight against the booth. "Now that you got me here, you tell me something. Why did you do it?"

He looks down at the table. "You know how these things are," he says, and he hears himself, and he knows that's wrong and that it makes him sound stupid, dull, unthinking. And if he didn't know it, her face would tell him.

"Why?" she says again.

"Because—" He can't say what he's thinking. Not to her face. Can he say they did it because they thought she was a bitch? Can he say that he followed Brig without thinking . . . and that he loved following him? Can he say that she was nothing to him but a pain-in-the-ass girl who was getting on their nerves?

They stare at each other. She's fingering the buttons on her coat. "Okay," she says. "I want to ask you something else. What if it happened to you? What if guys attacked you?"

"What?" He almost wants to laugh. What does this mean? Attacked him, like it happened to her? It wouldn't. It couldn't. "I'd fight them off."

"What if there were too many of them?"

"I don't know. . . . I'd get out of it."

"How? What if they were doing stuff to you and there was nothing you could do about it?"

"I'm too big. They don't mess with me." What does she want him to say?

"There're bigger guys than you," she says. "There's always someone bigger. Come on, Rollo, what if three big guys came up to you—what would you do, how would you feel?"

"You mean if they were fooling around, sort of

crowding me a little, sort of pushing in? I'd be looking for a way out, swinging at them—"

"I mean if they held you. Did what they wanted to you, anything they wanted to do." She's tearing a napkin into shreds. "What if they were doing that, and there was nothing you could do about it?"

He knows what she's after, he's not exactly dumb, no matter what she thinks. She's trying to make him step in her shoes, trying to make him think about guys on him, and him helpless, not able to do anything. "It couldn't happen," he says.

"But *if it did*? What then?"

He doesn't want to answer. He doesn't want to think about being helpless, but she's forcing him to think about it. Forcing him to think how humiliated he'd be, how his cheeks would burn and his heart pound a mile a minute.

"I'd crack them in the mouth, I wouldn't let them do it, I'd kill them, I'd say, *Get the hell out of my way!* I'd make them suffer, too." His hands clench. What is he doing? Why is he saying all this?

"This is stupid," he bursts out. He doesn't want to think about this. He doesn't want to talk about it. It puts a weak, watery feeling in his stomach. He stands up. He's not going to say another word to her. *Go to hell,* he thinks. He doesn't care if he ever sees her again.

– 29 –

"I want to go to my party in the library alone," Kara says.

"Your brother's going to take you," Rollo's father croaks from the bed. He's been lying there for the past two days with flu.

The New Year's party, an annual affair thrown by the town, is not something Rollo ever looks forward to, and this year he's especially uninterested. Aside from the fact that it's always massively boring—the decor is balloons, the menu is punch—there's something else Rollo doesn't like. A lot of teachers show up for the party. Why face them any sooner than necessary?

"I don't want Rollo to watch me," Kara says. "I

watch myself. I can be mature." She's wearing a pink dress with a swingy skirt, a pink ribbon in her hair, red satin, high-heeled shoes. "You can't watch me, Rollo. That's final. That's my final final. Mrs. Rosten says I'm mature, and I can say something final."

"Kara, can it. I don't want to hear you yakking all night long."

"Daddy! Did you hear that? Did you hear what my brother said?" She grabs her coat and walks out. "I'm going to my party by myself! That's final!" She pounds down the stairs.

"Go after her," his father says.

Outside, it's a clear cold night, and the moon is coming up in the sky. He catches up to Kara. "Here I am."

She pouts for a moment, then asks, "Do you think I look pretty?"

"Gorgeous. And very mature," he adds.

The party is taking place in a big meeting hall in the Highbridge Community Center. The library is lit up and there are people everywhere. Almost no kids his age, except some boys, clumped together in a corner, who are looking around, sneering. Probably the kids from the Cedars, the county juvenile home.

Rollo wanders around, eating cookies and occasionally checking on Kara. It's easy to spot her in the pink dress. She's okay, rushing around hugging and kissing people. He doesn't care as long as she stays away from the Cedars kids.

Suddenly he sees Mr. Maddox talking to Mr. Ferranto. Of all the people he would least like to meet, his principal and his English teacher are on the top of the list.

He crosses to the other side of the room looking for Kara. They can go home early. He finds her by the front windows, and she's with Valerie Michon. He hesitates for a moment, then he calls Kara. She and Valerie both glance up.

"That's my brother!" Kara's voice can be heard across the room. "Rollo!" She hugs his arm. "I have a new friend!"

"This is your brother?" Valerie says.

"Yes! I told you I had a brother. This is my brother, Rollo."

"What are you doing here?" he says to Valerie.

"What are *you* doing here?"

"Valerie is here with a friend," Kara says importantly. "She says a friend baby-sitter asked her to come."

"No, Kara, she's not a baby-sitter," Valerie says. "She's the lady I baby-sit *for*."

"I know, I know! Oh, this is such a good party. Everybody good is here."

Kara is all keyed up. Her cheeks are flushed, and she's talking at high speed. "It's the best party! Are you having a good time, Rollo?" She pauses for a second to plant a kiss on Valerie's neck. "This is my friend, Rollo, this is Valerie. Do you like her gorgeous blouse?" She touches the embroidery on the collar of the linen blouse Valerie is wearing. "I'll give you a kiss in a minute, Rollo. I know I'm excited. Do you want some punch?"

"Kara, slow down," he says. "We're going home now."

"No, I'm not going home yet! I want to talk some more to my new friend, Valerie. I have to dance, and I have to have some more punch. I'm going to bring you a glass of punch, isn't that nice of me?"

"Kara," he begins, but she runs off, and he and Valerie are left staring at each other. Then, abruptly, she walks away, too, leaving him feeling, well, the way you feel when somebody walks away from you, even if she's the person *you* walked away from the last time you saw her.

He wanders down the hall and looks into the darkened movie room for a while. Some figures with white ruffs and swords are on the screen. "Begone!" somebody cries. Or is it "Begin!"? He can't make sense out of what he's seeing. He keeps remembering the way Valerie looked at him a few minutes ago. Why does he care? He doesn't . . . but he does. It's confusing and stupid. He can't get straight about her. He would like to never, ever, think about her again. He would like to wipe her and what happened out of his mind.

But when he goes back into the meeting hall again, the first person he sees is Valerie, talking to a tall woman in a green knit suit. He steers wide and clear of her. He circles the room, looking for Kara. "Did you see my sister?" he asks a woman refilling the punch bowl.

"Do I know her?"

"She's Kara. If you know her, you know her."

The woman shakes her head. "I don't know her."

He walks around, but doesn't see Kara anywhere. He goes out into the hall again. Maybe she's in the bathroom. He knocks on the door. "Kara?"

Valerie is coming down the hall. Right. It must be his fate. "Are you going in there?" he asks, and then quickly, before she can take it the wrong way, "Would you check if Kara's in there?"

She goes in and then comes out again immediately. "No."

"She's not in there?"

"No."

"You sure?"

"You want to go in yourself and see?"

"Okay, I just wanted to be sure." He stares around the hall, frowning.

"What's the problem?" she says.

"I don't know where Kara is."

"Maybe she went outside."

"Why would she do that?" But it's a thought, and he's already on his way to the door.

The moon is behind clouds, the parking lot is dark. His eyes search among the shadowy lumps that are cars. "Kara?" he calls. Then he hears something, a sound, a wail . . . maybe a car radio. Maybe Kara. He thinks of the boys from the Cedars and moves fast between the angled cars. He's aware of Valerie behind him. He hears that noise again, a sound he can't identify. Is Kara crying? He races, his heart jostling in his chest, and he imagines . . . everything.

Clouds scud across the sky, the moon comes out and lights the edge of the lot, and there is Kara, dancing in the cold air, swaying and singing, holding out the corners of her dress.

"Rollo!" she says. "Look at me dance in the snow!"

"What are you doing out here?" he shouts. The relief is terrible, it makes him furious with her.

"I told you, dancing in the snow," she shouts back. Her cheeks are glowing. Her mouth is turned up in a joyful smile.

"You were supposed to stay inside!" Conscious of Valerie behind him, he tries to lower his voice. "I was worried, Kara. You shouldn't have done this without telling me."

"I always dance in the snow. Every New Year, I dance in the snow with Daddy. Don't you know that, Rollo, you dummy!" She twirls around. "Come and dance with me."

He takes a step backward. All he needs is to make a fool of himself in front of Valerie. "Kara, you've danced enough."

Behind him, he hears Valerie draw in her breath. "Danced *enough*?" she says, almost under her breath, almost as if she's talking to him. "How can anyone dance *enough*? Even for you, that's stupid."

"Kara!" he barks. "Come on."

"Valerie, Valerie," Kara sings, ignoring him, "you come dance with me."

"Oh, Kara, I'm not a very good dancer."

"Just one little dance," Kara pleads, dipping and swaying. "Please, please," she sings, holding out her hands. She doesn't stop moving for a moment.

Valerie steps into the circle of packed snow Kara has made with her stamping feet. She raises her arms, and begins awkwardly dancing, turning, throwing back her head.

Rollo stares at his sister and Valerie—one tall gangly girl, one short and round—two dark shapes shifting and moving in the half-light. Valerie is laughing and holding hands with Kara as they jump around.

When someone laughs, you want to laugh, too. And when someone dances, you want to dance with them. But Rollo can't do that. Well, he could—he could leap into the circle, he could spin and throw himself around, too . . . but he wouldn't. He wouldn't get out there and jump around. He might think of it, but it's not something he would do, not something a boy would do.

Now the two girls are going round and round, faster and faster, and they're humming, and their voices sound like the wind or water, something strange and half-wild.

And watching them, watching Valerie spin Kara

around, Rollo remembers that figure against the window. And in a series of flashes, like bursts of light, he sees himself moving toward her, he sees the three of them looming, moving in, he sees them like a wall rising, a wall darkening the light.

— 30 —

When Valerie returns to school after vacation, she
tries not to think about what happened on the third
floor. Just as she tries not to notice that, often, a
silence falls as she walks into a room, or that people
watch her a lot, or that remarks trail her down the
halls. She goes about her business, takes notes in
classes, does her homework, and talks to Janice, who
usually has something frivolous to say. And that's
good, because Valerie doesn't have anything to say.
There's a silence in her.

The second day she runs into Mark near the lab.
She's unprepared for how shaken she feels by the
sight of him. By his presence. "Valerie!" he greets
her, making her name into three words—Val Er

Eee!—like a little cheer. He pushes up his wire rims and leans in toward her as if he wants to hug her. She shrinks back, yet, curiously, what she wants to do, what her arms are nearly trembling to do, is to hug him. But . . . no.

"Are you going to tutor me this term?" he asks, nodding his head as if to say, *Sure you are!*

"No." she says.

"No?"

"No."

A little smile flickers over his mouth, is there, then gone. "Why not?"

He sounds angry, and that makes it easier. "I'm not tutoring anyone." She walks away, then back for an instant to say, "Sorry." And saying it, she is almost bitterly sorry, but so what? She doesn't trust him anymore. When you get down to it, what makes Mark Saddler different from any other boy? What does she even know about him, except that he has a great smile? Well, so does Rollo Wingate.

That day, she goes up to the third floor, because there's no other way to get into the art room. She takes the long way around. She avoids even looking toward the window at the end of the hall. She thinks she may take the long way around forever. The important thing is to get into the art room and begin working on her sculpture. But once inside, she doesn't do anything, just doodles aimlessly and stares at the clay.

The next day and the day after, it's the same thing. What's the matter with her? This was supposed to be her big breakthrough, the work that would be the best thing she'd ever done, that would be unique and wonderful, energetic, profound, and important. *What pretentious bullshit.* She sits on a high stool and makes little clay beads just in order to keep her hands busy. *I'm not ready yet to start it. . . . There's a right time to begin working. . . . You have to wait for the moment. . . . More bullshit and self-delusion.* Truth is that she's under a pall of anxiety and self-doubt unlike anything she's ever felt. In fact, not to be fancy about it, she's simply afraid.

Afraid she can't carry it off, that all her enthusiasm and inventiveness was poured out that morning when she doodled on a napkin and "saw" the sculpture as vividly as if it already existed. Afraid she's all wrong about the idea, that it's banal, that it won't be good, that people will laugh. . . . A thousand afraids, but no matter what words she puts to it, what it gets down to is that she's not doing it. She's not doing much of anything.

She feels tired a lot of the time. Her father notices

and asks if she has a cold. Instead of thanking him for his concern, she snaps at him, "Leave me alone!"

She feels more miserable than ever and lies on her bed, mentally tallying up her life. On a scale of one to ten . . . would she even give herself a four? She thinks of the whispers and looks. She thinks how in one more week the three boys will be back in school. She thinks about being mean to her father. She thinks about her sculpture—her non-sculpture—and that she's blown off Mark. No, not even a four. A three, maybe a two. She rolls herself in a blanket and allows herself to cry. Why not? She doesn't indulge very often in self-pity. And can't too long either, because Janice calls.

"Val, I feel like talking, and I don't have anyone else to call." A typical Janice remark.

"I'm not feeling too great right now, Janice."

"Me either," Janice says enthusiastically. "My nail polish won't go on right. It is so frustrating. Of course, you intellectual types don't think this is a significant matter in the universe. You could be right, but I happen to like smooth nail polish. It makes my life just that much nicer. I wonder if this has anything to do with my horoscope for the day? It said I should put fear behind and do what is right. Do you think that means I should buy some new nail polish?"

When Valerie hangs up, she sees that she's doodled Janice's horoscope in block letters. PUT FEAR BEHIND, DO WHAT IS RIGHT.

In the cafeteria, Denise Dixon pauses by Valerie's table. "Hi. Okay if I sit here?" Denise puts her tray down and slides into the seat across from Valerie. She unwraps a sandwich with long, red-tipped fingers, a precise and almost delicate operation in which the wrapping isn't crumpled but carefully folded. Valerie eyes her, wondering what's coming. She and Denise definitely don't run with the same pack. Not that Valerie actually runs with any pack, but if she did, it wouldn't be Denise's popular-girl-active-student-every-teacher's-darling pack.

All at once, Valerie remembers the last time she really noticed Denise—onstage, the day of the Christmas play. Denise had been good—what Valerie had seen of her. She cuts off this train of thought and concentrates on her egg salad sandwich. Her father baked the bread. It's sort of dry, and little pieces crumble onto the table.

"So," Denise says. "Um . . ." She leans across the table. "I heard what happened," she says, finally.

Valerie doesn't say anything.

A slow flush creeps up Denise's perfect skin. "I want to—I want to say how sorry—"

Valerie nods and bites into her sandwich. A rain of crumbs falls. She's going to have to talk to her father about making the bread moister.

"It's so horrible," Denise says. "Have you talked to anyone about it?"

What does she want, gossip?

"Have you thought about a therapist?"

Valerie can't resist. "I can always go to Mr. Ferranto's wife," she deadpans.

"Oh, no," Denise says. "You should get someone not involved in the situation."

The beautiful Denise hasn't got much of a sense of humor, Valerie realizes. The bell rings then, and Valerie gathers up her books and her crumbs and her soda can, but Denise is still sitting there, staring at her earnestly, as if she wants to say something and is searching hard for the words. Valerie stands up. "Well, see you," she says.

Denise gets up, too. "Val . . ." She takes Valerie by the arm. "I wanted to say . . . I want to tell you . . . the same thing happened to me," she blurts.

Valerie stares. Denise? Why her? She's not the type to go around stepping on guys' hands or egos.

"Last year," Denise says.

"Those boys?"

"No, not them, another one. He was grabbing me, he just kept grabbing my butt."

They walk out of the cafeteria together. Now Valerie is the one who wants to say something, but whatever she thinks of to say is inadequate. *How awful. . . . I know how you feel. . . . I'm sorry. . . .*

"I kept trying to avoid him, but I couldn't. I tried to talk to him and tell him to stop. He said it was just a joke. He pinned me one day in the hall. Nobody was around, and he—you know—"

Words are only words, and words can't carry the weight of what Valerie feels listening to Denise: such a tangle of emotions that it's days before she recognizes that mixed in with the by now familiar pain and humiliation is equally deep anger.

Rollo's father says, "You need to do something for someone besides yourself. You have to start thinking more of other people. What kind of community service do you want to do?"

"Community service?" This is something he's never thought about in his life.

"Who do you want to work with? Think!"

Rollo says the first thing that comes to mind, which of course is not thinking. "Old people?"

And that's why, every day for the next two weeks, he goes to the Senior Center and does whatever they find for him to do, which might be mopping a floor, washing dishes, or bundling newspapers for recycling.

During his two-week suspension from school, he also studies at home two hours every day, then goes to the library and sits there and studies for another hour. These are the rules his father laid down for him.

Most days, too, he meets Kara and walks home from work with her. And most days, now that they've returned, he sees Brig and Candy.

"You're white as a worm," Brig says the first time they get together. He and Candy are both tanned from having been in the sun. They have stories to tell Rollo, and the three of them talk a lot the first few days.

Rollo thinks at first that he'll tell his own stories about Valerie, but, faced with Brig and Candy, they seem too bizarre, too weird, too whimpy. He can imagine what they'll say if they hear how he pursued her and phoned her, how he nearly begged her to meet him. *You said you were sorry to her? Sorry for what? We didn't do anything, so how can you be sorry?* So, of all the things they talk about, there's one subject they avoid. They never talk about Valerie. They never talk about the third floor and what happened there that morning.

* * *

Rollo is trying to explain a strange experience he's had several times lately: he's awake, but feels almost as if he's asleep. Not awake, not asleep, just awake enough to know that he's waiting for something to wake him up from the sleep he's not sleeping.

Brig just laughs, but Candy's interested. "This happens in the morning when you wake up?"

"No, anytime. Walking down the street the other day. It's sort of a not-here feeling, like something is incomplete, like I'm waiting for something to be filled in."

"This boy needs a cold shower and a cup of coffee," Brig says.

Maybe he's right. Maybe a hit of caffeine or a surge of adrenaline will clear his head of the junk in it. A big clean wind to sweep out his brain, so he can start fresh again and make some sense out of everything that's been happening . . . and have some peace, too.

His father has some serious talks with Rollo, and that's pretty good. Well, it's not *good*; it's uncomfortable. He actually hates it every time his father says they should talk, but afterward he always feels better, somehow. And sometimes, after these talks, he has thoughts. He's never had actual *thoughts* before, ideas that come to him in well-phrased sentences, not that he can remember.

One thought he has is that he was a go-along. A follower. Someone who didn't ask questions or think for himself. It's kind of scary to have that thought; the only good part about it is that he has another thought: I'll never be a go-along again.

Nobody knows about these thoughts. Brig and Candy think he's the same old Rollo, just as Brig is the same old Brig, right down to hanging from his bar every morning for fifteen minutes. Maybe Candy's a bit quieter, but he's still Brig's best pal and the oil on Brig's troubled waters. So everything is more or less the same. Almost the same, Rollo thinks, almost like it was, yet he feels that something has shifted. It might be their friendship—he's not quite sure; it might be his life.

One afternoon, when they go over to the Racquet Club to work out, a new guy is behind the counter. The sleeves of his T-shirt are cut off to show his muscles, and he's wearing wire rims, like the ones he was wearing the night Brig and Rollo were at his house.

Rollo recognizes Mark Saddler right away. It takes

Brig a moment longer, just long enough for Saddler to say, "What are you doing here?"

"What I'm doing here is waiting for you to wait on me." Brig shoves his ID across the counter.

"Are these the other two clowns?" Saddler says, looking at Rollo and Candy.

Brig slams his gym bag against the counter. "Towel, boy!" he orders.

"Go to hell," Mark Saddler says.

Rollo puts his hand on Brig's shoulder. "Let's go down to the locker room."

"Let him give me my towel and tell me to have a nice day," Brig snaps.

"I wait on *people* here. You're nothing but a pimple on a flea's ass."

"I'll get you fired!"

Saddler grabs the counter like he's going to jump over it and strangle Brig. Candy and Rollo pull Brig away. When they leave the clubhouse later, someone else is at the desk.

– 32 –

Valerie has known all along that the three of them
were coming back to school: it was only a two-week
suspension. But she knew it the way you know things
with your head, not your guts. You know that it
would be rotten to have a car accident, but you don't
feel anything about it until you personally get
smashed up. You know you'd hate to have three boys
molest you, but you don't have a real idea what that
means until they do. And you don't know *at all* what
it's like to see those same three boys back in your life
. . . until they're there.

She sees the short one first, coming out of the gym.
The ringleader. Briggers. She gets such a shock she
almost backs herself into the wall. A bunch of boys

are with him. Are they talking about the third floor?
Her stomach lurches. She turns to avoid even passing
near them.

She sees the blond, freckled one next. He wings past
her in the hall without a glance. He either doesn't see
her or doesn't want to, which leads her to wonder
which is worse—to be visible to Briggers or invisible to
Candrella. In either case, it's like an erasure, isn't it?

At lunch, when she tells Denise this, though, the
other girl says, "Oh, no, Valerie, we can't let them
make us feel erased! We just can't. We can't allow
ourselves to feel erased." Helen Moore, a girl who's
always clowning around, rolls her eyes. "Better to be
the eraser!" She bends over, making exaggerated
erasing motions on the table. After a moment, Denise's face lifts in a little smile. She gets it.

Helen Moore is just one of the six or seven girls
who have gradually joined Valerie and Denise at
lunch every day. They've gotten a regular lunch club
going, and not always, but sometimes, one or the
other of them will lean in and start talking about what
Marcella Thompson calls third-floor things.

"Named in your honor, Valerie," Helen Moore
says, making a pious steeple of her fingers.

"I don't think that's funny," Denise says, until
someone pokes her and says, "Denise. Joke."

When they talk about third-floor things, mostly their voices are dry, they make wry remarks, but sometimes someone cries a little, telling about something she was afraid or ashamed to talk about before this. Something she wasn't completely sure was wrong, but which made her feel terrible and wonder what she had done to make it happen. Like finding out that her name was written with dirty graffiti all over the boys' bathroom, or being asked who she was going to bang this weekend, or having her blouse flipped up, or her bra strap snapped, or her skirt unzipped, or her legs commented on, or—but the *or*s seem endless.

"As many *or*s," says Helen Moore, "as there are boys in school."

"No, there are some good guys," Marcella says. She's tiny, blond, and fiercely fair. She looks at Valerie. "Don't you think so?"

Valerie shrugs. "Probably right." But she isn't convinced. She leaves the lunchroom warily, her eyes scanning ahead for Candrella or Briggers.

It's the end of the day before she sees the other one, Rollo, the one who can't leave her alone. He's hanging around the art room and gives her a smile, that sort of humble smile he's so good at. She doesn't stop, but she notices that compared to her hatred of the other two, she feels, well, almost an edge of friendliness toward Rollo. But that wears off fast.

"The thieves are back," she writes later in her journal, "free as birds. It scares me. I don't feel safe with them around. I keep remembering Janice's horoscope. Put fear behind and do what's right. I want to put fear behind. What do I have to do? Why can't I just forget them?"

But she knows why. There's no escaping them. They're right there in school. They're *there*, in her face. All the rest of the term, they'll be walking the halls, sitting on the steps, playing on the teams, talking to the teachers, opening and closing their lockers, going in and out of classrooms. They're going to be in her face, no matter what she does.

She sits back, her hands over her eyes. There *is* one thing she can do anyway, one thing that's right, even if it isn't about them. She lifts the phone and dials.

"Hello?"

"Hi . . . Mark?" She draws in a breath. "This is Valerie."

"Valerie," he says carefully. "What's up?"

"Oh . . . I've been thinking about a lot of things, Mark, funny things like erasers and horoscopes. . . . I might tell you about it sometime, but what I called for—I've decided to tutor you, after all."

"Why?"

No whoops, brays, or hoots of joy. Just a flat *Why?* Did she say it wrong? This isn't the response she expected. "Because I want to."

"Well, thanks, but it's not necessary. I'm getting someone else. We're starting next week."

She walks around her room, phone in hand.

"There are quite a few other people tutoring," he says.

"Right." She drops into a chair and nibbles frantically on her thumbnail.

"Of course," he says after a moment. "I don't know if anybody will do as good a job as you. . . . I learned a lot from you."

She sits up straighter. "I thought we were a great team."

"My sentence structure will never be the same again," he acknowledges.

"We could start tomorrow."

"Okay," he says.

"Does that mean yes?"

"Guess so." He allows a bit of enthusiasm to creep into his voice. "Anyway, I probably couldn't find anyone else as smart as you to help me."

"Just so long as you know it," she says.

— 33 —

"Valerie, how are you doing?" Mr. Ferranto says, as if she's just come out of the hospital.

"I'm okay." She sits down. He's called her out of her AP math class. She searches her mind to see if she's run afoul of any of her teachers lately.

Mr. Ferranto leans forward over his desk and looks at her searchingly. "Valerie. How are you doing?" he says again.

"Okay," she repeats. What is this all about?

"Valerie, I've been thinking about you. I'm aware of the gossip in school, I'm aware that you are in a sensitive position. You remember that I told you my wife is a psychologist. She's been helpful in alerting me to the issues here. She suggested to me that coming back to school might be trying for you."

"I'm doing okay." The warmth of Mr. Ferranto's gaze is confusing. Since that day when he expressed his "concern" for the three boys and then sprang them on her, she has felt a kind of suppressed loathing for him, as if he were part of what happened to her. Is it possible she misjudged him?

He sits back with his fingers steepled. "I have several suggestions to help you get past this difficult time with as little strain as possible. My first thought was that you might be a prime candidate for self-study. We could certainly arrange it. A lot of creative people are autodidacts, and that method of learning has great satisfactions, I'm told. You've scored brilliantly in all the national tests, you're in the top percentiles, but your marks have never been consistent, which suggests—"

"You mean stay home and study by myself?"

"Exactly!"

"But—"

He holds up his hand. "I know, that's extreme. However, another more realistic possibility has opened up." He shuffles some papers. "I've looked into the details of your transferring to Hoover High.

It's an excellent school with an outstanding record, and they would be delighted to have you."

"Go to another school?" she says, and she thinks what it would mean: first and best, leaving behind everything that reminds her of that day. Never having to see them again. Wiping the slate clean and starting over where no one knows what happened to her.

Then she thinks about being a stranger in a new school, the new-girl-on-the-block thing, not knowing anyone, not seeing Mr. Maddox again, not having Denise to sit with at lunch, or the other girls.

"Do you realize Hoover High has a nationally recognized art department? I've talked to the art people there and here, and we all have great hopes for you. This other school could be an opening, a real door to the future for you. I want you to think about it seriously."

He walks her to the door and says, "Valerie, we'll talk again. I want you to think about it."

When she reports this conversation to Janice, the other girl, not half as dumb as she pretends, says, "He wants to get rid of you. He's worried that something might leak out about the third floor."

"That's ridiculous. Everyone knows about it."

"They do and they don't," Janice says. "It's more gossip than anything. People aren't sure of what really happened. He'd like to get you out of the way, so everybody could forget about it."

"What's he afraid of?"

"Valerie! Dummy! He doesn't want bad publicity for the school."

"Oh."

"Oh! Right! The light dawns, huh?"

"You mean if I said something in public . . ."

"Right. You're a little time bomb, Val."

Hardly noticing that it's happening, Valerie begins working with the clay. She's not thinking about the sculpture but about what it would be like to be home, studying by herself. An autodidact. Flattering word. It is kind of tempting. Or is it? Does she want to retreat into her own little workshop, like her father? After a while she looks down and sees that she has made the first tentative movements into the scene of the mother and child in the rocking chair. Maybe that's when she knows for sure she's not leaving this school, she's not taking any of Mr. Ferranto's suggestions. It's her school—hers, not theirs—hers, as well as theirs.

When she comes out of the art room, Rollo is there

and thrusts a paper into her hand. "I said I'd give it to you," he mumbles and lopes off. She smooths out the paper. DEAR VALEREE, I LOVE YOU. WILL YOU COME SEE ME AT WORK I HOPE SO. YOUR NEW FREND, KARA WINGATE.

At home, she tacks Kara's letter on her bulletin board to remind her that nothing in life is simple. She puts it up next to the operative words from Janice's horoscope, which are pinned above a scrap of paper on which she has written in black Magic Marker, REFUSE TO BE ERASED. Slogans, admonitions, but they're helpful: they remind her of things, they tell her what she needs to remember.

"You know," Helen Moore says to Valerie the next day at lunch, "I've been thinking. You were really brave to tell as many people as you did what happened to you. I didn't want anyone to know."

Valerie laughs. "I was not brave. I was mad!" Then her nose feels hot and her forehead burns, and she realizes that since it happened, since the first moments of anguish and anger, she has not allowed herself to be that mad again. She has hated and feared and shuddered and shivered, but she has not been plain out-and-out burning mad. Mad that this could happen to her. Mad that the boys went after her as if she were game in a field and they were hunting dogs. Mad that everybody knows and nobody raised a fuss. Mad that Mr. Ferranto wants her out of the school. *Mad, mad, mad.* Mad enough to do something.

That weekend she writes a letter. She isn't sure who's going to receive it. Maybe the newspaper. Maybe the local TV station. She means to write the letter without undue emotion, to simply make clear what happened to her that day, and what has and has not happened since then.

Dear Editor,

I want to tell you about something that happened to me last December. So far, nobody has talked about it openly, in public. Whatever has been said about it has been said behind closed doors or in small private groups.

Here are the facts. I was on the third floor of my school. I was alone. I was looking out the window. And I was attacked by three boys.

We all know these things happen, but

somehow we think they're happening somewhere else to someone else. We read about things in the papers, see them on TV. Not here, we think. Not us. Not me. That's what *I* thought. Well, I was wrong. It was me. And since this happened to me, I've found out from other girls that it's happened to them, too.

How much is going on that we never know about? This is just one medium-sized school in one medium-sized community.

I want to forget this, but if nobody is saying anything, it's almost as if nothing happened. I admit, for a while I didn't want to talk about it, either. I thought I could put it away from me, not think about it, make it disappear from my mind. But that doesn't work. You don't forget. You don't stop feeling. It doesn't disappear.

If those boys had trashed the school and wrecked equipment, everybody would know about it. There wouldn't be any hush-hush. And it's pretty sure that they would have been punished with more than a two-week suspension. Some people would even call what they did a crime.

Why is what happened to me different? Am I less valuable than a room or a piece of equipment?

Why can't a girl be safe in her own school? Why can boys do what they did to me and get away with it? What are other boys thinking? Will the boys who attacked me do it again to some other girl? Will other boys get the idea that they can do this, too? Am I wrong to be worried for other girls? How do we stop those things from happening?

I hope you and your readers have some ideas.

Something bad happened that shouldn't have happened. Something that should never happen again. What should we do so that it never does?

Shouldn't a girl be able to stand in front of a window in her own school and be safe?

Yours truly,
Valerie Michon

– 34 –

Rollo's in the mall with Brig, killing time, waiting for Candy. "I'm telling you, I'm going to get it on the first try," Brig says. He's taking his road test tomorrow. "My brother had to take it three times. I'll save the family honor."

"Great." Restlessly, Rollo glances around. That's when he sees Valerie sitting at a table on the other side of the arcade. He begins to wave, then glances at Brig and drops his hand.

He's seen Valerie around school, of course, and once he saw her right here in the mall. But they don't speak, they've hardly exchanged a word since the New Year's party. He doesn't count the night she called to talk to Kara. He picked up the phone, she asked for Kara, that was it. It wasn't what you would call a conversation.

Brig goes off to get a soda, and Rollo, not giving himself a chance to think about it too much, walks over to Valerie. "Hi, it's me. Kara says to say hello."

"Oh, hi. Hello to Kara, too."

He shuffles his feet. "I'll tell her."

She's staring at him.

He clears his throat. "Well . . ."

"I was just thinking about you."

He drops into a chair. "Did you see me over there?"

She frowns. "I'm going public."

It sounds like something his father would say about stocks or an investment, but it's not what she means. He knows that right away.

"I'm sending a letter to the newspaper."

"Why?" His heart is thudding.

"Because people should know," she says, looking at him levelly. "Because I'm mad. Because you guys did what you wanted to me and you're home free. Because I don't see why I should go along with keeping it all under the table. I probably have about ten more reasons, but that's enough for now."

A letter . . . Will his name be in it? Even if it's not, a lot of people are going to know who she means. The thing will come out in a way it hasn't before. His father will be reminded. Kara will know. He thought it was over with, and now people will look at him and see a creep. They'll remember him as part of the gang who attacked her.

He looks down at his hands lying on the table. He remembers those hands on her, and for a moment it's very weird, like looking at two objects he doesn't recognize. He seems to hear Brig's voice. *That girl had it coming to her.* He must have said it himself.

"I wanted you to know before I sent the letter," she says. "Maybe it's foolish of me, but I think you're a little different."

"It'll just bring it all up again, won't it?"

"You mean for you? Yes. But for me, too."

His heart begins that peculiar thudding again, frightened, but in some way relieved.

"So it's all coming out?"

"Yes."

He nods. "It's coming out," he repeats. He stands up. "Okay," he says, and after that there doesn't seem to be anything else to say.

"Where were you?" Brig says, when he comes back.

"Talking to Valerie Michon."

"Michon!" Brig looks across the room, then at Rollo. "What the hell for?"

Rollo thinks of saying she's a friend, but that's not true. He shrugs and doesn't even try to explain. "I've got to get going," he says.

"What's the matter with you? We're waiting for Candy."

"No, I'm going."

"What's happening here, Rollo?" He looks across the room again. "It's got something to do with her, doesn't it?"

Rollo stands there. "It's complicated," he says. He fiddles with the strap of his knapsack, then slings it over one shoulder. "Brig." He holds out his hand. "Good-bye." After a moment, Brig slaps palms with him. "Good-bye," Rollo says again.

It really is good-bye, but he doesn't say that. Not now. He will soon. He walks away.